As a thriller novelist's comment on the fair and not so gentle sex in full cry, *Burning Sappho* detonates a megaton of Amazon emotions and intrigues.

That the characters here introduced as champions of Women's Lib carried to its wildest and most fanciful extremes are going to exceed the bounds of normal conduct is self-evident from the start. Murder and sudden death seem inevitable, and indeed they prove to be.

But that is not all, not by a long chalk. Under the bewitching powers of Sappho (best-selling authoress of *Female Slave*) the group known as *Sappho's Sisters* stages a march and demo, culminating in a bonfire of brassieres and an amazing mass denudation.

Behind these fabulous junketings a very great crime has been hidden and forgotten. It is gradually revealed.

The author of *A Queer Kind of Death* and *The Affair at Royalties* again demonstrates an eccentric talent that adds another dimension to the excitements of a strongly plotted, vividly funny crime novel.

By the same author

Burning Sappho

GEORGE BAXT

'The isles of Greece, the isles of Greece!
Where burning Sappho loved and sung,
Where grew the arts of war and peace,
Where Delos rose, and Phoebus sprung!
Eternal summer gilds them yet,
But all, except their sun, is set.'

George Gordon, Lord Byron
Don Juan

MACMILLAN

SBN 333 13714 0

First published 1972 by
MACMILLAN LONDON LIMITED
London and Basingstoke
Associated companies in New York Toronto
Dublin Melbourne Johannesburg and Madras

Printed in Great Britain by
RICHARD CLAY (THE CHAUCER PRESS), LTD,
Bungay, Suffolk

*For Phyllis Jackson
and Elaine Greene,
provided they can get
this book published*

I

'*Murderess!*'

The voice needed oiling but the eyes were fully stoked, circular blazing furnaces that threatened Belle Grady with instant immolation.

'*Killer!*'

The mouth from which the accusation emerged like a poisoned dart was like a jagged ugly wound. Willi Horn's cheeks matched the combustible colour of her eyes. Her fingers held Belle's victim by the nape of its neck, the trembling hand caused the two small bells attached to the pink ribbon around its neck to sound like the advent of an ice cream vendor.

'A sweet innocent kitten!' Willi shrieked. There was almost a question in her voice as though perplexed by the thought that all nine lives could have been consumed by one twist of the neck. Belle sat in the window seat of the cramped living room with arms folded and legs crossed, reflexes in control in case she'd have to dodge the dead animal. Willi was backing away slowly like a pitcher about to wind up for the toss.

'Why'd you kill it?' Each word was tear-drenched though Willi's eyes were dry.

Belle unfolded her arms, uncrossed her legs and leaned forward, each hand tightly clutching the edge of the window seat.

'One of its dainty little paws tore a ladder in my stocking and my calf so I grabbed it by the throat to give it a good shaking.' She paused and shrugged. 'I thought cats were made of sterner stuff.'

'You always hated Marlene.' Willi's voice was now a husky whisper and Belle inwardly applauded the effective transition. It brought back transient memories of past seductions.

'Why don't you throw it down the incinerator?' Belle had always been the practical one.

'*Oh!*' With the unoccupied hand Willi clutched her breast as though expecting to find the hilt of a knife protruding.

'Are you planning to stuff and mount it and put it on your dressing table along with your kewpie dolls?'

The hand holding the dead kitten was now stretched over Willi's head, her face convoluted in a heterogeneous look of horror and astonishment. 'You *hate* me!'

Belle examined the fingernails of her left hand as she spoke. 'I don't hate you at all, sweetie. I happen to love you very much. But that took a bit of time, if you'll give pause and remember.' She indicated the furry corpse with a quick jerk of her head. 'I could have learned to love Marlene if she hadn't been so damn pushy.' She elevated her left leg. She studied the coagulated blood and the three unattractive ruts, sufficient evidence as far as Belle was concerned in any case of murder in self-defence. 'Supposing I get an infection from *this*.'

'It would serve you right!'

Belle lowered the leg as she spoke. 'Your loyalty is about as reliable as the dollar.'

Willi was now cradling the dead kitten in her arms. 'Poor little baby. Poor little kitten. Poor little Marlene. Your uncle Belle was just jealous, that's all. Just jealous because you were a birthday present from Sappho Yannopoulos.'

Belle groaned.

Willi's monologue continued like an undammable flow of lava. 'Uncle Belle thinks Sappho Yannopoulos is trying to steal me away from her.' Belle snorted. 'Uncle Belle is jealous because she's not as smart and as rich and as sophisticated as Sappho Yannopoulos.' Belle guffawed. 'Uncle Belle is jealous because she'll never write a best seller like

Sappho Yannopoulos. She's so jealous she won't even read *The Female Slave*.'

'It's a load of crap.' The words were like sandpaper being drawn across an open sore and Willi's head shot up.

'It's *brilliant*.'

Belle's eyes narrowed. 'If you think so much of that kitten why don't you carry it by your teeth to Central Park and give it a proper burial.'

'Poor ittoo Marlene.' Willi was stroking it with an index finger, taking her usual sadistic joy in provoking the vulnerable Belle. 'Sappho Yannopoulos said you were as cute and as fluffy and as playful as I am.'

'You're about as cute, fluffy and playful as a porcupine in heat.'

Willi's chin began to quiver as once again she held the kitten by the nape, swinging it slowly like an acolyte holding the censer. 'Uncle Belle will never be a guest of David Frost or Johnny Carson or banter witticisms with David Susskind. Uncle Belle will never attend a reception at the White House or have a personal guided tour through the palace of Monaco by Princess Grace. Uncle Belle is uncommitted and useless and Sappho Yannopoulos says she must have lots of splinters from straddling fences and Uncle Belle feels I'm slipping away from her because I'm one of the most important men in *Sappho's Sisters* and now I'm Sappho Yannopoulos's private secretary and I spend my weekends at Sappho's magnificient estate on Long Island and ...'

Willi was startled by the sudden clap of thunder. At least then it sounded like one to her. It took her several seconds before she realized it was the impact of Belle's right fist when it connected with her quivering jaw. She was sprawled on the floor still clutching the kitten when she heard the second clap of thunder. The room trembled as though a fleet of sanitation department trucks were passing by. It was another spate of seconds before Willi realized the second clap of thunder was a door violently slamming shut, and then she realized the succession of drumming from the hallway was not a military tattoo, but Belle's heavy tread as she raced down the staircase away from their third floor walk-up.

Willi released her grip on the dead kitten, struggled to a sitting position, felt her jaw and then ululated in a mixture of pain, anger and self-pity. Now holding her jaw with both hands in fear that it might break loose and fall on the floor in shattered fragments, she got to her feet and staggered to a wall mirror.

'Look what's she done!' she screamed at her dishevelled reflection. Her jaw was blue and badly bruised and felt dislocated. She spun about and stared at the dead kitten. 'Look what she's done!' A volcano of fury, she rushed across the room, levitated her right leg and sent the furry corpse hurtling against the far wall with a drop kick that would have brought envy to the face of a professional footballer. Then her ferret eyes searched the room for another target. They found Belle's framed diploma from the Policewomen's Academy. She tore it from its hook on the wall and flung it with hurricane force against the opposite wall. Slivers of glass rained on the Morris chair beneath. A lamp was pulled from its socket and added to the debris. A plaster statue of two nude goddesses in a compromising position was added to the debacle followed by an assortment of ashtrays, a crystal fruit bowl and a variety of paperbacks haphazardly stacked on the coffee table.

Then backing away to get a satisfying perspective of the damage, she stepped on the dead kitten and leapt forward with a startled shriek. She turned and stared at the dead animal.

'Oh, my poor Marlene!' she howled. 'Ain't us girls suffered enough?'

Straighten up and fly right, Belle told herself as inferno-like emotion jet-propelled her tall, slim, beautifully propor-

10

tioned body along West Tenth Street towards Fifth Avenue. Fill your lungs with the fetid air of Fun City. Play hopscotch with the dog faeces decorating the sidewalk like chocolate chips in a tollhouse cookie. There's remaining anger to vent and perhaps some unsuspecting masher or junkie or purse snatcher will make the fatal mistake of attacking you. A judo slash, a karate cut or even an old-fashioned hammerlock on an arm twisted behind the back while you slowly crack each finger singing 'This little piggie went to market' etcetera.

Get hold of yourself, girl. Keep your cool. It's taken guts to accomplish what you've made of yourself and you did it on your own. You went as far as you could go as a policewoman and now you're one of those rare chosen creatures, a licenced private female detective. They don't make too many like you baby and that stupid Willi should have known that by now. Piss on Sappho Yannopoulos. Piss on *Sappho's Sisters*.

Belle turned into Fifth Avenue and pointed her nose towards Washington Square Park. The weather was uncommonly mild for October and the sun setting over the arch reminded her the shabby city was still capable of its fleeting moments of beauty. She needed to think with a drink at her elbow but in unfamiliar surroundings where the chance of running into an acquaintance at the bar or being hailed from a booth was minimal. I've passed the Great Divide. I've crossed the Rubicon. I'm thirty. There's got to be more to it than this. Shacking up with another broad isn't my scene. I said I'd try anything once and I tried it and I've had it. I didn't mean to kill that effing kitten.

'Hey lady!' an urchin shouted after her, 'your leg's got blood on it!'

Belle quickened her pace while cursing under her breath. She turned into Eighth Street, found a shop, purchased hosiery and changed into them in a curtained alcove. By the time she was entering Washington Square Park steering herself towards Bleecker Street, she was humming in quick, nervous snatches. There was counterpoint from a group of hippies at the fountain strumming guitars and singing a freedom song.

Did I mean to kill that effing kitten? Do I really love Willi Horn or is it that I hate loneliness? Why don't I phone the old precinct and see if Tony Mingus wants to take me to dinner tonight? Big bull of a Tony, with your cauliflower ears, your mashed nose, your scars, your ham fists and that lazy deceptive slouch that opens into a man mountain when you straighten out. By me you're beautiful. Why didn't we try to make it? Because I froze up, that's why.

'Maybe you should see a shrink, baby, huh?'

Maybe I should do a lot of things, Belle told herself. She scrubbed phoning Tony. Maybe later but not now. You can't talk girl problems with Tony. Whatever he thinks about Willi he's kept it to himself. But she could envision him growing red choking with laughter over the sock on the jaw. Tony appreciated the release of violent physical contact. He could rhapsodize about it. It was the closest he came to being a poet. But would he wax lyrical over a strangled kitten?

Belle felt her knees grow weak and managed to make it to a bench before she fell. She sat with her head lowered, eyes shut and hands clasped tightly on her lap.

I strangled a kitten.

'Oh, my God,' she whispered. There was heat on her cheeks and she realized it was tears. She fumbled in her jacket pocket and extricated a handkerchief from under her key ring and money clip. She wiped her eyes, blew her nose, and from another pocket brought out a pack of cigarettes and matches. Her first drag was a long one and she held it until her lungs began to revolt.

Marlene! What a hell of a name for a cat. Belle watched a tired old hot chestnut vendor push his converted baby carriage past her and thought of her father rising at five a.m. to scrounge for a day's work at the Brooklyn shipyard.

12

Then a parade of ill-assorted women goose-stepped into her memory, the motley crew of 'aunts' her father established in residence over a period of fourteen years following her mother's defection when she was a toddler of five. Poor old Pop, thought Belle with a sigh and then another drag on the cigarette, twenty stories was one hell of a fall, the hazards of window washing on a defective scaffold. Dear old Mom, in Belle's dim memory the earliest exponent of women's liberation. Where you been these past twenty-five years? Did you ever recognize my picture in the papers? That was a great shot of me sailing into that student's riot at Columbia. That was a cute caption under the picture. *Belle Of The Brawl*.

Cat killer.

And Belle chuckled mirthlessly. Another quirk of memory brought back Little Essie Morelli from the old neighbourhood, the kid who seemed to do nothing all day but catch flies and pull their wings off.

'So what?' said Little Essie's mother in defence of the fairest of her brood. 'Lotsa kids ketch flies and pull off da wings!' But the other kids don't eat them.

Belle resumed walking with head down and hands jammed into the jacket pockets. It was over a year since she had resigned from the Metropolitan Police Force to open her own detective agency. She was gratified and touched by the number of clients recommended mostly by former police associates. She hadn't realized she commanded that much respect and affection. Nothing big mind you, but enough to pay the bills with enough left over to pay for her constantly dwindling supply of nylons.

God damn that cat!

As she rounded a corner into Bleecker Street, the overhead street lamps came alive. There's no use for twilight in this twilight zone, Belle reflected. A shabby street with shabby bars and shabby people with shabby minds and shabby facades for pizza palaces in which only the royalty of the lower depths reigned. She paused under the grim canopy of a funeral parlour to reconnoitre for a likely oasis. She espied *Buster's Bizarre* which was new to her and undoubtedly to Buster on the opposite side of the street, squeezed between an antiques shop, *Past Imperfect,* and a faggot men's shop, *Sartorso.*

A double scotch on the rocks was served her with eager dispatch by a bartender whose hirsute countenance gave her a fleeting urge to feed him peanuts. The stool on which Belle perched was an oval island between bar and plate-glass window affording her a complete view of the interior and the street, a throwback to her police training. Always sit where you can see it all. There was enough wall between bar and plate-glass window to provide a back rest and she slouched against it as she lit a cigarette. She had the place to herself and wasn't sure if it was sanctuary or exile. She sipped the scotch and the familiar comforting taste was like a long-awaited kiss.

'How's the drink?' It was the bartender who spoke. Belle wondered if his mouth was where it ought to be.

'The drink's fine. How long you been open?'

'Little over a week.' Belle thought she detected college in his voice. 'It'll get busier in a little while. We're beginning to catch on.'

'I'm sure you will,' said Belle with encouragement, 'everything's catching in this neighbourhood. Are you Buster?'

'No I'm Seymour. Buster doesn't come in till late. Would you like another ice cube?'

'To do what?'

'You had a peculiar look on your face when you sipped the drink like it wasn't cold enough.'

'I was thinking of somebody who's cold enough.'

Sappho Yannopoulos.

Belle wondered if Seymour was smiling as he retreated to the opposite end of the bar and a copy of *New York* magazine. *I was thinking of somebody who's cold enough.* Belle reflected on the night five months ago when she and

14

Willi first met Sappho. The invitation to Pat Drake's cocktail party was as unexpected as an inheritance from a distant relative. Pat was a free-lance article writer who'd placed a piece on Belle in one of the better magazines much to Belle's and probably Pat's surprise. The usually acidulous Pat had managed to keep a civil tongue in her typewriter and Belle was pleased and flattered by the result. She'd sent Pat a note telling her as much and several weeks later the invitation arrived.

'But what'll I wear?' Belle fretted when Willi insisted they attend.

'Armour,' suggested Willi and Belle finally settled on a buckskin pants suit she'd purchased in a giddy moment one weekend in Easthampton. When they arrived at Pat Drake's apartment in a brownstone on East Fiftieth Street, the living room was a bouillabaisse of women. Pat Drake greeted them effusively in a voice that sounded like the business end of a tea kettle at full boil.

'I'm *so* glad you came!' Belle introduced Willi. 'I'm so glad you *both* came.' Pat's acicular nose was on a level with Belle's chin. Belle was frozen in position, afraid to move for fear Pat's nose would draw first blood. 'Sappho Yannopoulos is here. I'm doing some publicity on her new book. *Female Slave*. Out next week. Like to read it? You've *got* to. I've a carton of them in my bedroom. I'll get Sappho to autograph a copy for you. It is *divine*. Bestsellersville. I can *smell* it.' Belle could see she was more than adequately equipped for that. 'I mean that book really speaks for *us*. Kate Millet? Forget it. Germaine Greer? Alice in Wonderland revisited. Anne Koedt? Carry *her* back to West Vagina. This one's the *powerhouse*. Fifty thousand first printing. They expect it to really *explode*.'

Pat ran interference for them across the crowded room until they reached the fringe of a circle of women surrounding, Belle was positive, the deity herself. Belle recognized Liz Bancroft, the television newscaster who stood with a highball in one hand, the other hand loosely around the shoulders of a massive, middle-aged woman Belle would have cast as a prison warden. Pat whispered in Belle's ear, 'Sappho's dying to meet you. She read my piece on you and absolutely flipped. In her eyes you are the *completely* liberated woman.' Belle silently disagreed, Pat's grip on her arm feeling like a shackle more indigenous to a chain gang. 'Liz,' Pat hissed, 'this is Belle Grady and her friend . . . er . . . Trader Horn.'

'Willi Horn,' corrected Willi with her best party smile.

'I'm so *bad* on names. And Belle, this is Babe Lustig.' The prison warden turned and for the first time in years, Belle felt like cowering. The face and its features confronting her had obviously been chiselled on a stolen tombstone. The hair was steel grey and closely cropped. The only thing that distinguished her from the late Wallace Beery was a pair of pearl earrings.

'I am happy to meet you,' said Babe Lustig as she thrust forth a block of cement Belle quickly recognized as a hand. The grip was strangely gentle and Belle reassured herself if the emergency ever arose she could take Babe Lustig in three falls.

'You're so much handsomer than your pictures,' said Liz Bancroft. It wasn't a compliment, it was a weather report. Each word was clipped, sharply enunciated and void of emotion. Belle introduced her to Willi.

'I watch you every night!' gushed Willi, sounding like a voyeur defying police detection.

'What a clever outfit,' said Liz to Belle blandly.

'I'm glad you like it,' replied Belle, 'it makes me feel like Daniel Boone.'

'Well, my dear, aren't all of us here pioneers?'

Pat interjected quickly. 'This isn't so much a cocktail party as the first meeting of *Sappho's Sisters*.'

'We're the first recruits,' added Liz.

'Ah!' said Belle. 'Of course. It sounded at first like a family reunion.'

Babe Lustig moved in front of Belle. 'But we *are* a

family. We are the family of liberated womankind. No longer shall we be denied our economic, political, psychological and *sexual* independence.' She sounded like the loudspeaker announcement of a plane departure at Kennedy.

Belle felt a tug at her sleeve. She turned and saw a chipmunk. 'Hi there,' twittered the chipmunk, 'I'm Pauline Potter. I'm Sappho's secretary. She wants to meet you.' The eyes blinked as she spoke and when she was finished, four chipmunk teeth remained exposed. She was slightly over five feet tall sporting a dutch bob that had obviously been set by a mangle. She wore a plain white blouse and a black skirt that Belle decided would have been stylish in a girl's reformatory. She sounded twenty, but looked forty. Belle recognized the type. They attended twice-weekly lectures at the New School for Social Research, walked other people's dogs, paid admission only to foreign films and survived on yoghurt.

'I'd love to meet her,' said Belle.

'Come on then,' said the chipmunk grabbing Belle's hand. Willi patted her hair and followed.

Sappho Yannopoulos sat in a pale green easy chair delicately fingering a string of perfectly matched pearls. She wore a beige, sleeveless shift that barely covered her knees. Her legs were crossed and shapely. Her skin was ivory white and her eyes were deep blue and penetrating. Her raven hair was smartly coiffeured. Her mouth was perhaps a bit too broad and the lipstick was cleverly applied to underemphasize the minor defect. She was an exotic and imposing woman and Belle was openly impressed.

'I've been looking forward to this,' said Sappho warmly after Pauline finished the introductions. Her voice was narcotic. Belle decided it had taken years of cultivation. She also wondered if she was expected to kneel at Sappho's feet. There was no room to sit. As though reading her mind, Sappho nudged a girl parked on a footstool. The girl, who was dressed like a shepherdess but looked as though she had

17

just eaten her flock raw, reluctantly gave way to Belle.

As Belle awkwardly settled on to the footstool, Sappho leaned forward and said, 'My dear, I just adore your mind.'

'I haven't spoken it.'

'*There!*' said Sappho as Belle imagined Columbus must have sounded on sighting land. '*There's* what I admire in you! *I haven't spoken it.* Just like in Pat's article. Cool, self-contained, highly individual, your own woman!' Her radar detected Willi. 'And who is this?' Belle introduced Willi who sank to her knees next to Belle, perhaps, thought Belle, in the hope that Sappho would touch each shoulder with a sword.

'I'm a great admirer of yours Mrs. Yannapoulos,' said Willi with a bludgeoning sycophancy that made Belle go red with embarrassment.

Sappho leaned forward and purred as she gently chucked Willi under the chin, 'I can see where you're going to be a great asset to the sisterhood.' Her eyes moved from Willi to Belle. 'Did you arrive together?'

'We did,' said Belle blithely, 'which tells you everything.'

'Oh, you are marvellous! Marvellous!' Sappho's hands were waving about as though in a rush to dry freshly painted fingernails. 'Pat! Pat! Where are you?' Pat moved forward. 'You caught her perfectly! *Perfectly!*' Then to Belle, 'You're too *brilliant* to be a policewoman!'

'Thank you,' said Belle softly while suffering the discomfiture of the spotlight.

'She's not a cop any more,' said Willie in a rush, 'didn't you know? She's got her own office now. She's a real private eye.'

Sappho cocked her head in Belle's direction. 'You must love that kind of work. But somehow,' she added with a note of sorrow that rang as true as a statement from Ananias, 'I seem to see a great waste of administrative genius.'

'Sappho, I'll graze anywhere I find grass.' She turned to

Pat. 'Any chance of getting a drink?'

'Oh, my heavens!' cried Pat, '*what* a hostess! Mavis!' she shouted over her shoulder. 'Mavis! On the double!' A solid black woman in a severe uniform materialized as though a lamp had just been rubbed. She took Belle and Willi's orders, asked if anybody else wanted anything, and narrowed her eyes slightly as she was impatiently waved away by Sappho. With her other hand Sappho snapped her fingers and Pauline swiftly produced a cigarette and lighter.

'Now tell me Bale,' (and as Belle drained her glass at *Buster's Bizarre* she unconsciously winced at the memory of Sappho's pronunciation of her name), 'tell me what you *really* think of the women's liberation movement.'

Belle folded her arms and examined the ceiling. She inflated her cheeks and held the unflattering pose for several seconds, then exhaled and found a smile for Sappho. 'Well to tell you the truth, Sappho, I haven't given it much thought.'

'I don't believe it.' Sappho pouted. 'I don't believe that at all. I can *tell* from Pat's article you have very *strong* opinions about our revolutionary movement.'

'It's not all that revolutionary, honey,' said Belle as Mavis returned and served the drinks. 'If you've read your history,' and Belle didn't miss Sappho's flinch, 'you know it goes back centuries. For my money, Virginia Woolf said it all in *A Room Of One's Own* and that was over forty years ago. Ever read it?'

'I'm afraid not.'

'I'll lend you my copy if you like,' said Belle and sipped her drink. Behind her, she didn't see Liz Bancroft smiling slyly. She did see the subtle change of expression on Sappho's face.

'I'd like to *give* you a copy of my book. Then ... *then* when you've read it, I'd like us to meet and *really* talk.'

The chipmunk started chattering. 'I'll get a copy right now. Pat's got loads in her bedroom!' She scurried away as though pursued by a fly swatter. Belle wished she had taken

Tony up on his invitation to go bowling.

'Sappho's right,' piped Willi, 'a person's nothing without some kind of commitment. I mean, if there had been any hope of your becoming Commissioner of Police, would you have quit the force?'

'Bravo!' exclaimed Sappho and patted Willi's head. Belle wondered if a golden corona might appear but none materialized. There was only a glow on Willi's face she hadn't seen since their first night together and looking back at the moment, Belle realized their relationship was then steering into a stormy sea.

'Tell me, kitten, what do you do?' Sappho was leaning towards Willi with an elbow on her knee, a flat palm propping up her delicate chin and looking like a cold cream advertisement.

'I'm a secretary in a public relations office,' said Willi with pronounced distaste.

'And no hope of advancement.' Willi's occupation was an infant's minor bruise a loving mother was promising to kiss away.

'Oh, there certainly isn't,' agreed Willi forlornly, 'I'm just another machine like the typewriter or the Xerox.'

'Machine!' Sappho clasped her hands, closed her eyes and arched her neck. 'That is the putative word for woman's position in the masculine hierarchy.' The head moved forward as the eyes flew open. 'Machine! Robot! Instrument!' Belle envisioned a surgeon barking for instruments at a delicate operation, knowing full well the patient was doomed. 'We shall abolish that. We shall have the equality that is rightfully ours. Man's sexual, economic and political hegemony shall be a thing of the past, and you, little kitten,' her finger's gently stroking Willi's willing cheek, 'you shall become a moving force in this crusade. I promise you that.' She looked over Belle's head and barked, 'Babe!'

As apocryphally happened when Moses commanded the parting of the Red Sea, Sappho's circumvallation of hand maidens made way for Babe Lustig who came forward like a thresher through a sea of wheat.

'Babe.' Sappho's voice was grave. 'You will take this kitten's address and phone number.' Belle was twisting a buckskin fringe around an index finger. Willi's eyes were misting with joy. 'You will create a post on our staff for Miss Corn ...'

'*Horn.*' The chipmunk was hidden behind Babe Lustig, clutching book and ballpoint pen.

'Horn ... of course. ...' Sappho favoured Willi with a smile that spoke of tax-deductible benevolence. The chipmunk edged her way around the formidable Babe Lustig like a cat burglar on a narrow parapet.

'Here's the book and a pen,' she clackety-clacked, and Sappho took them, opened the book and there was a churchly silence as she painstakingly wrote an inscription. Belle was unsurprised when the book was handed to Willi. Belle got to her feet and raised her glass.

'Here's to you, Sappho.'

The expression on Sappho's face was that of a revivalist minister welcoming a fresh convert.

Belle continued succinctly, 'Because you can certainly make a souffle out of a pile of crap.' She drained her glass, shoved it at the convenient chipmunk, wondered which karate chop she'd make should Babe Lustig make a threatening move, and when it wasn't forthcoming, pushed her way through the circle of women and sixty seconds later marched belligerently along East Fiftieth Street in search of the nearest bar.

Seymour the bartender at *Buster's Bizarre* asked the question three times before Belle realized he was speaking. 'Would you like a refill?'

'Oh,' said Belle dumbly, and shoved the empty glass towards him.

Seymour stood prepared. He dropped two ice cubes into the glass and then inundated them with scotch.

'I'll have the same,' said Liz Bancroft placing a bag of

21

groceries on the counter and drawing a stool closer to Belle. 'Whatever thought you've been deep in, honey, it's not worth the scowl on your face.'

Belle shook her head and managed a weak smile. 'I'm sorry. I didn't see you come in.'

'I saw you through the window.' She had a cigarette in her mouth and detonated a slim-line lighter. 'I live around the corner. Just been doing my shopping. Christ, the price of beef's so high they must be feeding the cattle L.S.D. How you been?'

'Surviving.'

'Watching the big parade tomorrow?' She exhaled a perfect smoke ring.

What parade? wondered Belle, and then the fog cleared. Protest march. Sappho's Sisters. Fifth Avenue. Remove brassieres on the steps of the Forty-Second Street library. That'll expose a sea of red-eyed monsters. 'I can't miss it,' said Sappho, 'they'll be doing their big number across the street from my office.'

'I'm covering it for the tube, of course.'

'You don't sound terribly enthusiastic.'

'I'm a little bored with Sappho.'

'What happened to that pioneer spirit?' Seymour had served Liz's drink and remained in attendance. She shot him a look that promised instant castration and he hastily retreated. Liz snorted and Belle wondered if it was a delayed reaction to her question or a rude comment on Seymour.

'Pioneer spirit my ass. How clever of you to remember. How many months ago was that party at the Drake thing?'

'Approximately five.'

'And how's the little kitten?'

'I strangled it. Oh ... you mean Willi.'

'I was hoping you meant Willi.'

Belle shifted towards Liz. She was finding her suddenly interesting. 'I gather you don't much favour my bitter half.'

'Minions are always a pain in the ass. Since replacing

22

poor little Pauline as Brunhilde's second in command, she exudes that fetid air of self-importance usually associated with a false pregnancy. If I didn't know better I'd say she was a prick, but I articulate better when my copy writers provide the material.'

Belle folded her arms and with some difficulty crossed one leg over the other. 'I think you're doing just fine.'

'You know,' said Liz after a quick gulp of scotch which had obviously been preceded by other drinks at some previous watering hole, 'I could only tolerate such a crashing bore if she was incredibly rich and fatally ill. Are you about to take a sock at me?'

'I wouldn't risk being thrown off the premises. I need this drink.'

Liz's face was half turned to Belle and she saw half of a warm and friendly smile. 'You know something Belle, I really hate my job. I left a lot of unidentified corpses and battered bodies in the wake of my hurricane rise to my present exalted position, and I wish I was capable of the resurrection. I'd trade it all in for one effing son of a bitch I could call my own. Here's one lady that wishes there was a wolf at the door.'

Belle said wryly, 'I see dangerous signs of revisionist tendencies.'

'Oh, honey,' she said with a disdainful wave of hand, 'that was just a performance at that party. I was just doing my job. I had to play it cool. Research department. You know, when Pat introduced us, I said to myself, and I talk to myself a great deal because it is the rare moment when I receive intelligent answers, I said to myself, now here is the ideal cannon fodder for Sappho's armoury. And girl,' she bellowed, 'you sure proved me wrong. I have dined *out* on your exit line for *months*.'

'I wish I'd known that,' said Belle softly.

'Why?' asked Liz cocking her head and fixing Belle with a quizzical eye.

'Because it was the Ice Age revisited around our pad for

23

many weeks after.'

'Listen,' said Liz edging forward cosily, 'we barely know each other, but I think I recognize a half-sister. How can somebody who obviously has as much on the ball if you'll pardon the expression as you have put up with some pallid little fluff who undoubtedly was born out of idle curiosity.'

'Girl, you *do* go on.'

'It's the secret of my success, but keep it to yourself. Oh dear, I think I'm getting pissed.'

'Why do you hate Willi?'

'I don't hate her, I *deplore* her. I see a lot of Sappho and her gang, and I'll continue seeing her as long as she's news. And she's rich enough to afford to keep making news. You know she's really got old Nikos Yannopoulos stewing on that yacht in the Aegean. She took him for millions, you know. But he doesn't mind that, he's got plenty left over for chewing gum. It's basking in her reflected glory, the re-minder to the world he exists. He doesn't like spotlights. He likes to work in the dark. She's brought him too much attention, even if indirectly. He wishes she'd fold her tent and steal away, but I got news for him, that'll be a long time coming. And I got news for your weeping Willi, when it does come she'll be out on the trash pile along with the rest of them. You know,' she you knowed again while signal-ling for fresh drinks, 'Willi is very high-handed and very officious and very obnoxious and one of these days I'm going to send her a poisoned choir girl.' She began using a thumb against her breast bone like a battering ram. 'No-body keeps *me* waiting.'

'Say, aren't you Liz Bancroft?' It was Seymour again.

'No, sonny, I'm her twin sister and I'm wanted by the police.'

Belle signalled him to move off and he walked away with shoulders slumped, another idol shattered.

'Why don't I help you home?' Belle suggested gently.

'Oh, darling, I'm not *that* far gone.' She indicated her glass. 'This is just for starters.' She reached into the bag of

24

groceries and found a small purse from which she pulled a piece of tissue and dabbed at her nose. 'Oh, it's not just the Sapphos and the Willis of this world that turn me off. It's life itself.' She jammed the tissue back into the purse and redeposited it into the bag of groceries. 'The studio won't let me go to Vietnam. They say it's no place for a woman.'

And Belle exploded with laughter. Liz's chin dropped as the irony of her own statement struck her and joined Belle. 'Hoist by her own petard!' she shouted and then put a friendly hand on Belle's shoulder. 'You were looking perfectly miserable when I found you.'

Belle's lips tightened as she stirred her drink with the swizzle stick and then said, 'I strangled a kitten.'

Liz shook her head to clear it. Belle told her the story.

'I am sure that has very deep psychological connotations,' commented Liz at the conclusion of Belle's narrative, 'but frankly, being allergic to kittens and for that matter anything feline, I say full marks for you and to hell with it.'

'I hope she's not there when I get home.'

'The kitten?'

'Willi. I hope she's not there.'

'She won't be.'

'You're so sure.'

'Five gets you fifty.'

Belle smiled. 'I'm glad you came through the door. Let's have dinner some night.' The invitation took Belle by surprise and pleased Liz.

'I'm glad you asked. I'd like that.' She rubbed her palm against her cheek. 'Actually, the boyfriend's walked out.' Belle said nothing. 'For the past three weeks it's been Siberia time. The hell with it. Tell you about it sometime. Gotta get home. Gotta pull myself together.' There was an absurd smile on her face. 'Got to face those damned cameras at eleven tonight. Gotta cover that damned protest march tomorrow noon. Gotta do all the things I spent years dreaming of doing, and it's all so much dross.' She was fumbling in the purse.

Belle stayed her hand. 'These are on me.'

'Oh, come on now.'

'On me, I said.'

'Thank you. I shall reciprocate very soon. You can reach me at the studio and I'm sure you're in the book.'

'Under Grady comma Belle private investigations.'

Liz winked and left.

Shortly after her departure, Belle paid the tab and went home. She climbed the stairs slowly to the top floor apartment. She found the strength to insert the necessary keys into the three double-locks on the door, and entered the dark apartment. She flicked the wall switch and went white at the sight of the attendant carnage. She began trembling with rage and hoarsely shouted 'Willi!'

Willi was gone. Belle found empty drawers in the dressing table and bureau and empty clothes hangers in the closet. Belle slammed the closet door shut and shouted 'Good riddance!' She stomped from the bedroom across the living room into the kitchenette and pulled open the refrigerator door. She swung open the freezer compartment and stifled a shriek.

There the kitten had been laid to rest.

II

'*Bale* strangled the kitten? My birthday gift to you? Little *Marlene?* But this is a *schrecklichkeit*!' The occasional betrayal of foreign accent in Sappho's speech underlined the horror of her reaction to the ghastly information imparted by Willi. She was lying face down on a masseur folding table in the second floor bedroom of her town house on West Eleventh Street, a blue towel modestly draped across her shapely behind. Babe Lustig was delicately kneading her waist like a master pastry chef preparing dough for a classic eclair.

Willi was sitting on a mink covered ottoman dripping tears into a glass of port. 'I tell you Sappho, I've never been so frightened in my life.' Every four words were punctuated by a dry sob, 'It's like she really meant to strangle me and not poor Marlene. But that's not the half of it. For no reason whatsoever she socked me in the jaw.' Her head shot forward. 'Look at me!'

Sappho shook her head and clucked her tongue sympathetically. 'I have an excellent cosmetic that will camouflage the discolouration. It was created for me by a myopic beautician in Athens who unfortunately was assassinated by the new regime when he turned his talents to gelignite.' She directed her mouth over her right shoulder and barked, 'Enough Babe, enough.' Babe's hands froze in mid-air. 'Willi, be a dear and fetch my dressing gown.' Sappho indicated a diaphanous creation of peacock feathers draped across a Hepplewhite chair. With a sweep of her hand the towel fluttered to the floor, and in two agile movements belying her fifty-three years, stood posed on the thick carpet awaiting the dressing gown like Venus on the half shell. Willi affectionately draped it around Sappho's shoul-

27

ders. Babe watched through narrowed eyes as she folded the table and carried it to a closet.

Hands akimbo, Sappho paced the floor like a bird of paradise gliding across an everglade. 'I suppose you have nowhere to go on such short notice.'

'No,' said Willi forlornly.

'There are plenty hotels,' suggested Babe.

Sappho paused in front of a full-length mirror and examined herself like a curator who'd recently uncovered a lost Titian. Past her reflection she saw Willi standing with head lowered, biting her lower lip. What a nuisance, thought Sappho, what an incredible nuisance. If I offer her shelter tongues will start wagging and there are enough tongues wagging as it is. Certainly that wretched Pauline has been spreading gossip about us, but Willi is certainly an improvement on Pauline if only in appearance. How I loathe ugliness and how deceptively I tolerate it. Nikos with his troll's face and body, Babe who looks like an armoured tank that survived the Battle of the Bulge, eighty per cent of my sisterhood who could start a boom in cosmetic surgery if only they would submit.

Babe's voice penetrated Sappho's meditation. 'The committee is waiting downstairs. Have you forgotten the parade tomorrow?' Only 'parade' emerged musically, demonstrations of any sort bringing back to the mountain of a woman joyful memories of another era when she goose-stepped through the streets of Berlin blissfully unaware of the occasional whispered comment she looked like Herman Goering in drag.

'The committee. Oh my God. There is so much to do and so little time in which to do it.' She crossed to Willi and put an arm around her shoulders. 'Blessed Juno!' Sappho said to the ceiling, 'she's trembling like a blender. Babe we simply cannot deny her a bed at least tonight. Prepare the Aphrodite suite and after the parade we will consider the alternative. Now, Willi, my precious seraph, we have had enough tears. I cannot establish you in per-

28

manent residence because it would be bad for my image.'
Babe was humming atonally under her breath, aware she
couldn't carry a tune even if it had handles. She was
lumbering to the door like a monolith magically invested
with life. With her hand clutching the doorknob, she turned
to Sappho.

'What about the other situation?'

Sappho's face darkened as she moved away from Willi.
'We'll discuss it after the meeting.' Babe nodded gravely
and left.

Willi meantime had dried her eyes and squared her
shoulders. 'Will you want notes taken?'

'What? Oh yes ... notes. ...'

'What's wrong?'

'Nothing that concerns you, Willi. It's a personal matter.'

Willi pouted. 'One thing you can say for Belle, she
always confided in me.'

'So nice to know she has a virtue. Oh, do go fix your hair,
and powder your face and change your suit and stop looking
like some effigy any angry mob forgot to burn!'

'Well, what are you mad at *me* for? I didn't do anything,
did I?'

Sappho exhaled in exasperation and crossed to her ward-
robe muttering imprecations under her breath in a variety
of tongues. As she slid back the door to select an appro-
priate costume for the meeting, she looked over her shoulder at Willi and snapped, 'For crying out loud will you get
going?'

Willi clenched her fists and stomped a foot. 'I can't stand
it when you're mad at me!'

Through Sappho's clenched teeth there debouched, 'I am
not angry with you I am simply preoccupied with more
important matters than your private life and your emotional
emergency.'

Willi's eyes widened with fear at the thought of a possible superannuation. 'You're not trying to get rid of me
too, are you?'

'Get rid of you? What are you talking about? I just wish you'd get out of here while I get dressed. Now stop making a nuisance of yourself, Willi. I realize you've been through a traumatic experience with Bale and that bloody kitten, but there are more important matters at hand. There are twenty sisters waiting in the salon downstairs including Lady Molly Burke who's flown in from London *especially* for tomorrow's demonstration. I suppose I should wear tweed.'

'I'm not spending the night here!'

'Suit yourself.'

'I'm going to a hotel.'

'As you wish.'

Willi was at the door. 'I'm going back to Belle.'

'A commendable display of bravery.'

Willi clenched the doorknob. 'I'm losing my respect for you.'

Sappho removed a tweed suit from the rack and turned to Willi. She said coldly, 'I'm glad you're beginning to know your own mind.'

Willi's chin quivered. 'Don't you love me any more?'

'You've had your fair share of my affection. I told you months ago it could never go further than that. You're behaving very badly. Now if you promise to be a good girl, I'll buy you a fresh kitten.'

'I don't want any god damn kitten.'

'Would you prefer a mongoose?'

Willi giggled.

'That's better,' said Sappho with a wan smile. 'Now if you promise to be a good girl, we'll have dinner alone up here after the meeting.'

Willi looked down abashedly at her tennis shoes and asked plaintively, 'By candlelight?'

'Yes, dear,' Sappho acquiesced wearily, 'and then we'll drink acquavit and listen to Chris Connor records. Feel better?'

Willi rushed across the room and flung her arms around

30

Sappho. 'I love you! I love you the best of everyone in this whole wide world!' She peppered Sappho's face with kisses. 'You know I could never not respect you Sappho, you know that don't you? Gee whiz I'm the luckiest kid on the block to be close to someone like you. That's how I feel Sappho, that's how I really feel. Do I have to move out tomorrow?'

Sappho moved Willi gently to one side as she crossed to her dressing room. 'You know as well as I do the lesbian element in our revolution is beginning to weaken its impact. It's frightening away the ordinary housewife and the other heterosexual women who would otherwise strengthen our forces. We *must* woo that silent majority. My lovely book is accomplishing part of that job, but I'm receiving too many letters questioning the incidence of our homosexual supporters. We need more feminine women!'

'Like Ann-Margaret?' squealed Willi eagerly.

'It wouldn't hurt.' Sappho was wondering if it would be politic to eschew her brassiere for the committee meeting. 'Anyway, that explains why we can't live together, *kapish*?'

Understanding and assurance wreathed Willi's face as she punched the air like a shadow boxer. 'I'm with you all the way, lover.'

Babe Lustig swept back into the room like a cannonball smashing a barricade. 'The committee is getting impatient!' she shouted. 'Some of them have to go home and cook dinner for their husbands!'

'All right all right all right!' cried Sappho. 'Willi, go get ready!'

Willi fled the room. Babe followed her to the door and slammed it shut as Sappho emerged from the dressing room buttoning a lace blouse. 'Willi is becoming a problem,' said Babe.

'I agree. She's turned into quite a handful.' She sat at her dressing table, picked up a hairbrush and neatened her coiffure. 'What's missing from the files is more important. Damn Pauline!' She dropped the hairbrush and covered

31

her face with her hands.

'Damn Nikos for sending that letter.'

Sappho dropped her hands and stared at herself in the mirror. 'Damn them all.' She turned and smiled at Babe. 'But we shall overcome. Haven't we always.'

'Always!' thundered Babe and then raised her beefy hands over her head, clenched her fingers tightly and shook them victoriously.

Belle sat in front of the television set watching an antique John Wayne western. As always, she was rooting for the Indians. She bit into a stalk of celery as the phone rang. Eyes glued to the set, she fumbled for the instrument, found it, and propped it between neck and shoulder. 'Hello,' she growled.

'Hullo tiger.'

Belle sighed with relief. 'Tony, I've been hunting all over town for you. You said you were going bowling so why weren't you at the alley.'

'Ah, some spook Panther cut up his wife when he realized their white kitten wasn't his own. We were chasin' him all over Central Park and finally caught him takin' a piss in the lake. It's still early. You wanna hit some pins?'

'Come over here. I've got something to show you.'

'At last.' Belle smiled despite herself.

'It's not that nice. I have to talk to you. I have to really talk to you, Tony.' She was shouting over the din from the television set.

'So stop yellin' a'ready, I'm comin', right? What pitcher you watchin'?'

'Tony, will you please stop horsing around and get over here?' Her voice broke.

'Hey tiger, you ain't goin' woman on me all of a sudden? Come on baby, yuh still my favourite cop.'

'Stop it, Tony, or I'll drown the mouthpiece.'

'I'll be right dere. Get out the ice cubes.'

'I can't.'

'You mean they're stuck? That's what you need me for?'
'You stupid wop,' she shouted, 'will you get over here?'
'I'm dere a'ready!'

Belle slammed the phone down and stared listlessly at the remaining celery. She stared at the television screen and it was a blur. 'Oh hell,' she whimpered and crossed to the set and turned it off. She wiped her eyes with her sleeve and then glanced at her wristwatch. It was not yet nine o'clock. Still early enough to hit some pins. She felt a sudden chill and her teeth began to chatter. Pull yourself together, she admonished herself, pull yourself together. You told Liz Bancroft, she understood. Tony will understand. Tony will get the frozen corpse out of the freezer. Tony's had a long history of dealing with dead bodies. Even her own.

Pauline Potter scurried along Ninth Avenue to the building where she shared an apartment with Michaela Lorimer. She had the feeling she was being followed and kept looking over her shoulder like a frightened fox gauging the distance from its baying pursuers. She drew her leather jacket tighter around her body and broke into a trot. As she passed a dark alleyway, a garbage can crashed and Pauline yelped. She hadn't wanted to work overtime but this was a new job and she wanted to make an impression. Good jobs weren't all that plentiful and it had been six weeks of unemployment between her unpleasant departure from under Sappho's umbrella to her new status as filing clerk for a producer of pornographic films. Stinking ungrateful Sappho. Crusader for women's liberty, hah! If I told all I knew, if I told the real story, hah! A drunk lurched out of a doorway and stood wavering in her path. Pauline froze. Pauline's heart pounded with pain. Her breath came in short gasps. The drunk took a shaky step towards her, lowered his head as though attempting to bring her face into focus. He rubbed his eyes and stared again.

'Go 'way,' he mumbled, 'go 'way and I won' drink any more, I promise.'

Pauline emitted a sob and skirted past him. So what if I'm not pretty, she consoled herself as she ran, I've got more important assets. I take shorthand and I can type seventy words a minute and I'm a good housekeeper, I know that because Mike never complains. She glanced quickly over her shoulder to see if the drunk was still there. She saw him clutching a lamp post, shaking his head back and forth as though refusing some private entreaty. Pauline quickened her pace. She reached the entrance to her building, unlocked the door, slammed it tight behind her and then raced up the stairs and unlocked the door to the apartment.

'Umph! Oooof! Urrffff! Owffff!'

Michaela was exercising with her bar bells. She stood five foot eight inches in gym sneakers and weighed one hundred and sixty pounds which was mostly muscle. For three years she'd been a reigning queen of the roller derby, her lethal elbows notching several dozen broken ribs and fractured breast bones. At the Tokyo Olympics she'd made an admirable impression at javelin throwing and shot-putting and if a mouse were to scurry across the floor, she'd collapse in a dead faint. Pauline had seen it happen.

Pauline was leaning against the door gasping for breath. Michaela caught sight of the pathetic figure and lowered the bar bells to the floor.

'You look awful, Paul. You want some yoghurt?'

Pauline shook her head no and found the strength to remove her jacket.

'You got a phone call.'

'Who?' Pauline managed to squeal.

'Pat Drake. She says to call her back. Number's on the pad.'

'Pat Drake? What does she want with me?' She crossed to the telephone table and stared at the number carefully pencilled on the pad. 'I haven't spoken to her in months.'

Michaela was standing in front of a mirror flexing her right arm and admiring the muscular bulge that resulted.

'She's waiting for your call. She said she'd stay in till you called.' Michaela reversed position and now favoured her left arm. 'Something to do with something she's writing about that Sappho fruit.' Michaela liked neither Sappho nor liberated women. Her secret ambition since childhood was to be the master of a trireme and beat hell out of the slaves manning the oars. Her second secret ambition was to go fifteen rounds with Cassius Clay.

Pauline sat by the phone and pondered the number on the pad. 'It's a trick. I know it's a trick. It's got something to do with all those terrible phone calls I've been getting from Babe Lustig.'

'Yeah, I'd like to meet that one too,' said Michaela gruffly, 'head on.'

Pauline began whimpering. 'I'm so frightened. Mike I'm so frightened. They think there's something I know that could be a threat to Sappho.'

'You said you know a lot of things about Sappho that ain't so kosher.'

'I know! But if I knew *which* thing they were frightened of, I'd promise not to tell!'

Michaela was stretched out on the floor doing push-ups. 'The trouble with you is you're too defenceless. You should start working out at the gym with me ... twelve ... thirteen ... fourteen. ...'

'Mike, what'll I do?'

'How can I give you an answer if I don't know the problem. Phone the Drake fruit and see what she's got on her mind.' She did an amazingly agile backflip on to her feet and started deep knee-bending exercises. Pauline lifted the phone and slowly dialled.

In her pink and white bedroom designed by Rupee Keeler, the half-caste Hindu temple dancer who turned to interior decorating when she developed a permanently stiff neck, Pat Drake was reclining on her pink velvet divan. She was receiving a pedicure from a delicate young man kneeling at her feet who only did house calls. He was applying a

35

delicate shade of coral polish to her toenails while doing a fair imitation of Edith Piaf prior to her death. When the phone rang, Pat swiftly raised an index finger to her lips and the young man abruptly cut his vocalizing in mid-note.

'Pat Drake here,' she said briskly into the mouthpiece. 'Oh, Pauline angel, I thought you'd *never* get back to me! How you been sweetie? Well let me tell you what it's all about. I've got this assignment from *Exploit* magazine to do this series of articles on Women's Lib and I simply need your *help* on Sappho.' A sober expression covered her face. 'What do you mean is this some kind of a trick? What's bothering you? Don't you want to help?'

Michaela was walking around the room on her hands while Pauline held the telephone like a live hand grenade. 'I don't trust any of you. Ever since I got elbowed out of my job by that little bitch Willi, I have lived in constant fear of my life!'

'Now, who'd want to hurt you?' Pat gushed as a tiny bell rang in her brain alerting her to the possibility of an even better story than she'd been hoping to write.

'*They* do, Sappho and Babe. They're afraid of something they think I know.'

'Such as?'

'I wish I knew!'

This girl is paranoic, thought Pat, yet on the other hand ... 'Now listen sweetie, I really called because I sincerely need your help in gathering my facts. I promise you this is no trick. Why don't you come over to my place tomorrow night after work. ...'

'I'm afraid.'

'Well certainly not of *me* I should hope. I'm all woman and a yard wide!' The delicate young man pursed his lips in an expression corroborating Pat's statement as he studied her hips.

Pauline nervously ran her fingers through her bristly hair as she spoke into the mouthpiece. 'I'm afraid to go anywhere but *home* after work. I ... I think I'm being followed!'

'Lucky you.' Then Pat resigned herself to the inevitable. 'Look sweetie, I am perfectly content to go over to your place. I mean I ordinarily loathe going below Forty-Second Street because it gives me the bends, but for *you* I'll make an exception. Now why don't you phone me just as you're leaving work, and then I'll hop into a cab and scoot right down.'

Pauline slowly repeated her address and hung up. Michaela was doing splits to strengthen her thigh muscles. Her eyes were riveted to Pauline. 'You didn't tell me nothing about being followed.'

Pauline folded her hands in her lap. 'I didn't want to alarm you.'

'You gotta be joking. You know I ain't afraid of nothing. From now on I pick you up at work and see you home, okay?'

'Oh Mike, it's so far out of the way from the gymnasium.'

'So? What's my motorcycle for? But try not to work too late, will you? I got plans for tomorrow night.'

If Mike's got plans, thought Pauline, there must be a full moon tomorrow night. That means Eighth Avenue between Forty-Second and Fiftieth, with Michaela like a gourmand confronted by a large box of chocolates and carefully pondering the assortment until selecting one with a soft centre. 'You promised to stay away from those black whores.'

'Why don't you mind your own business?' Michaela had formed her body into an arch to strengthen her stomach muscles.

'After that trouble the last time you said you'd never go back there again.' Pauline's voice had started low but ended on a screech. Michaela now sat with her legs crossed, an ominous look on her face, and an index finger the size of a cucumber pointing at Pauline.

'Didn't you promise not to give me any more trouble?'

'But you *also* promised!'

'Do I have to beat you up again?'

Pauline cringed. 'You promised you wouldn't do that again either. Haven't I been good to you?'

'You been great. The service around here is perfect. But you gotta learn to mind your own business. Do I have to remind you the day I left home when the old man asked one question too many, it took four doctors twelve hours to set his bones.'

'I worry about you.'

Michaela held up a fist. 'Pauline, I'm warning you. Worry about yourself. You're the one with the problems. Now get your ass moving and rustle us up some grub. I stole a side of beef this afternoon.'

'Real cute and stiff as a board.' Tony Mingus was staring at the dead kitten while he groped for a can of beer. Belle had taken five minutes to explain the incident to him before showing the *corpus delicti*. 'What da hell, tiger, it was just an accident. Jeez, do you know how many of these they gas a day over at the pound? Enough to feed hungry Packerstan.' He tore off the beer can tab and took a swig. 'Gimme a paper bag. I'll t'row it down the incineerater.' Belle found a bag in a cupboard and gave it to him, and then returned to the living room. The sounds of Tony prying the frozen kitten loose from the freezer compartment sent a chill up her spine. She poured herself a stiff scotch. As Tony emerged from the kitchen, the phone rang. Belle crossed and picked it up watching Tony crossing the room holding the paper bag in front of him with distaste.

Belle had difficulty finding her voice.

'Belle Grady? Is that Belle Grady?' The voice at the other end was shrill and vaguely familiar.

'Yes,' said Belle huskily.

'This is Pauline Potter? Do you remember me? Pauline Potter?'

The chipmunk.

'Yes Pauline.'

'Listen,' said Pauline with urgency, 'this is a business call. It's very important I see you right away.'

'I can't right now.'

'Oh gee why not?' Tony had returned, shut the door and sat opposite Belle nursing the can of beer after winking and signalling Belle thumbs up for a job completed.

Belle couldn't resist. 'I'm holding a wake.'

'Oh well gee I'm sorry. Well ...' there was a pause to indicate Pauline was doing some thinking, 'maybe sometime tomorrow can I see you? My lunch hour is between twelve and one. Can you see me between twelve and one?'

'Sure. Come at half past. We can watch the big parade from my window.'

'What big parade?'

'*Sappho's Sisters*. Are you that much out of touch?'

'I wish I was. I forgot all about it I'm so frightened. It's Sappho I got to see you about. I think my life is in danger.' From the franticness at the other end of the phone, Belle wasn't too sure her prospective client would survive until the next day's appointment.

'Calm down, Pauline. Are you safe at home?'

'As safe as home will ever be. Where's safe in this day and age? You notice how much I trust you, knowing you and Willi ...'

Belle interrupted sharply. 'Be one of the first to know. Willi has left my bed, bored.'

'Oh.' There was another pause. 'Well you're well out of it if you don't mind my saying so.'

'Pauline, let it wait till tomorrow.'

'Okay, okay. Please be there, huh?'

'I never miss an appointment.' She heard some garbled words of farewell and then the line went dead.

'What was that all about?' asked Tony.

Belle shrugged. 'The plot sickens.'

Preoccupied, Belle drained her glass. Tony leaned forward, the beer can dangling between thumb and forefinger. 'Come back to me baby, I'm feelin' awful lonely all of a sudden.' He watched Belle place herself at the edge of the window seat. 'I ain't seen dat look on yuh face since dat night I tried to get yuh in duh hay.'

'Jesus Christ when the hell are you going to stop with that phony "dese" "dem" and "dose". This is me! It's Belle! You don't have to put on acts with me!'

Tony hadn't realized the bomb on the window seat had so short a fuse. 'Okay kiddo, relax. "Dese" "dem" and "dose" fits fine with my mashed nose and my cauliflower ears. What was that phone call all about?'

'I'm not sure,' she said in a strained voice. 'I'll know more tomorrow. It was a girl named Pauline Potter, the one Willi deposed in Sappho's favours.'

'What was that bit about being safe at home?'

Belle repeated Pauline's end of the conversation. Tony took a swig of his beer and then scratched an ear lobe. 'She some kind of a nut case?'

'I don't know. I only met her once before at a cocktail party at Pat Drake's, you remember, that first time I met Sappho.'

Tony nodded, and then a silence fell between them. Belle was pondering the two signs of disaffection against Sappho she'd encountered that evening, Liz Bancroft and Pauline Potter. She'd read how Fidel Castro dealt with disillusion among his ranks, but found it hard to believe Sappho could resort to such internecine methods. After all when her childhood friend Gussie Moskowitz resigned from the *B'nai B'rith*, the worst that happened was they removed her name from the list of choice locations for theatre benefits. She heard Tony overemphasize clearing his throat and looked up. She apologized for her silence.

'It's okay, tiger. You know I get the same when I'm trying to piece together a dismembered body. I'm on that protest detail tomorrow.'

Belle knew Tony Mingus was too valuable an asset to the

police department to be delegated a Women's Lib protest march. 'They expecting some kind of trouble?'

'Well you know how it is tiger,' said Tony as his legs sprawled forward, 'if a couple of hundred broads threaten to remove their brassieres on the steps of the Forty Second Street Library, that could be sniper fodder. Christ, what the hell's this world coming to? I mean really what's going to become of us?'

'I don't bother thinking about that Tony because it's happened. What we are now is what has become of us.' She stood up briskly and slammed the empty glass down on an end table. 'Are we going to sit here philosophizing all night or are you taking me to dinner. We can go dutch.'

'Up you,' growled Tony as he struggled to his feet, 'no broad pays her own way with Tony Mingus. Where you wanna eat?'

A wicked look played on Belle's face. 'How'd you like a preview of what you're going to have to face tomorrow?'

'Ah for Chrissakes not one of them topless joints. Who wants flabby tits hanging over my shrimp cocktail.'

'I'm taking you to the hangout,' said Belle checking herself in the wall mirror, '*Checkpoint Charlotte*.'

'Oh yeah?' Tony's face lit up. 'I thought that joint was off limits to guys.'

'Not when escorted by a lady. The food's good believe it or not.' She tripped over broken glass. 'Damn Willi. Will you look at this place?'

'Maybe Willi's coming back to clean it up,' said Tony with an impish expression.

Belle shot him a deadly look. 'That's about as likely as being served a pork chop on an El Al flight. Come on, let's get out of here. This place is giving me the creeps.' She moved past him to the door and he caught her arm and gently positioned her facing him. Lightly he kissed her forehead and then they embraced tightly, Belle's head resting on his ample shoulder. 'Tony, where've you been all my life?'

'Waiting.'

Pat Drake was a psychedelic vision in pailleted brown blouse, velvet green hot pants and silver sandals. It was half an hour since her conversation over the phone with Pauline Potter and she'd been contemplating seriously the implications she thought she'd heard between the lines. The delicate young man who'd applied the pedicure was seated cross-legged on the divan sipping daintily from a glass filled with chipped ice and green mint. He'd been watching Pat circling her gold princess phone for ten minutes looking like a hyena sizing up its prey. He shot a look of impatience at the ceiling, gripped his waist with his left hand, then narrowed his eyes as he shot verbal darts from between cupid's bow lips in a totally unexpected baritone. 'Are you going to make that damned call or are you going to kiss it in hopes it turns into your prince?'

Pat braked to a halt and glared at him. 'You hush your mouth Malcolm. I have a feeling I'm on to something but I'm not quite sure how to handle it.'

'Why don't you let it simmer for a couple of hours while we get some dinner. I *feel* like I'm about to *expire*.'

'The only way they'll get you is with a silver bullet,' said Pat with a haughty sniff.

'Charlotte's will be *jammed* by the time we get there. We'll *never* get a table now. Oh God,' his eyeballs rolled up and showed white, 'the thought of all those dikes tearing into roast beef with their bare fingers. *Why* do you insist on *eating* in that place?'

Pat was pacing again and muttering 'Should I? Shouldn't I? Should I? Shouldn't I?'

'For God's sake you had two hours of that Greek loudspeaker at that committee meeting. . . .'

'She's only Greek by marriage. I'm going to call.' She lifted the phone and dialled. With a sigh, Malcolm lay back on the divan with one hand cushioning his head. 'Babe? It's Pat Drake. I'd like to speak to Sappho. I haven't caught her

42

in an awkward moment, have I?'

Babe stared at the mouthpiece of her phone with distaste. 'Madam is dining.'

'Oh dear. Well maybe *you* can help me.' Babe clutched her phone with both hands as though by some miraculous stroke it would turn into Pat Drake's neck. 'I've been talking to Pauline Potter and she's absolutely *hysterical* with fear. She says she's being *threatened* by you two. Now what's *that* all about. I mean Pauline Potter of all people!'

'Bah!' growled Babe, 'she only imagines those things.'

'Pauline Potter isn't *capable* of an imagination,' Pat stated flatly. 'She says *you've* been making the threatening phone calls. I mean she's in such a state my dear, I fear she might regress to Simone de Beauvoir.'

Babe Lustig's face was a sheet of metal. 'Do not concern yourself with this. It is a private matter.'

'Let me speak to Sappho!'

'Madam is dining.'

'Oh for God's sake this'll only take a minute!'

'I will inquire if Sappho wishes to speak with you.' She pressed the hold button and buzzed Sappho's suite. She knew better than to continue sparring verbally with Pat Drake. She loathed the woman but secretly admired her tenacity. And she was valuable to Sappho.

In Sappho's bedroom, the light on the intercom on the desk glowed red. Willi obliviously continued dishing chocolate mousse into her mouth while Sappho took the call. 'Yes, Babe?' She listened for a few seconds with closed eyes and then said, 'All right I'll speak to her. Stop fretting. I can handle this.' She pressed the button on the intercom that connected her with Pat Drake and managed to muster some warmth in her voice. 'Good evening, dear. Yes the meeting did go beautifully. Yes wasn't Lady Molly a delight.' She drummed her fingers on the desk top with impatience. 'Now what's this nonsense about Pauline?' Willi looked up with interest as her tiny tongue wiped chocolate mousse from her lips. 'Oh that's a lot of nonsense,

Pat. Nobody's threatened to *kill* her.' Willi pushed her plate aside and sat tensely clutching the edge of the table. 'Look dear, it's simply a matter of some private papers removed from the files in the East Hampton house. Well who else but Pauline could have taken them? I said they were *private* papers dear which means they concern only *me*.' Sappho shot a 'heaven help me' look at Willi and wondered why Willi had gone so stiff. 'I didn't realize they were missing until just a few days ago. I haven't been out to the house in weeks, you know that, we've been too busy.' Sappho endured the chatter at the other end for fifty seconds and then interrupted. 'All right, dear, all right. You talk to her tomorrow night and see what you can do. No this is *not* a matter for the police, it is strictly private and I want it kept that way. All right dear, all right, thank you for calling.' She slammed the phone down and buzzed Babe. She picked up the phone again, swinging it like a mallet pulverizing the air. 'Where the hell is she ... Babe? Come up here. I said *now* damn it!' She slammed the phone down again, crossed angrily to a sideboard and poured herself a brandy.

Willi found her voice. 'If that Pauline is up to anything I'll kill her!'

Sappho's eyebrows arched as she turned to the table. 'Would you, darling? Would you really?'

III

Lady Molly Burke sat regally erect in the back seat of the taxicab as though the streets were lined with cheering subjects. It was approximately nine thirty p.m. and almost two hours since she had attended the meeting at Sappho's town house which she had found 'charming' 'edifying' 'stimulating' and to herself, a crashing bore. The majority of Sappho's supporters had struck her as rejects from a Vassar daisy chain and she was disappointed no time had been alloted for a private talk with Sappho. She sniffed the white carnation in the lapel of her grey suede jacket and almost lost her balance as the taxi lurched up the ramp leading on to the West Side highway. 'Easy old girl,' she shouted. Flo Hopper grinned at her passenger in the rear-view mirror.

'Sorry hon,' rasped Flo, 'that truck jockey ahead of me's driving like he's on an acid trip.' Flo sounded as though she had once mistakenly gargled with a solution of lye. 'First trip to New York?'

'Oh heavens no.' She stared out the window at the docked ocean liners, the Hudson River and the New Jersey shoreline and wondered why so many New Yorkers loathed their own city.

'I hope you know what you're heading into.'

Lady Molly's laugh was satin. 'I'm not in the sense you wondered when last the hair had been washed. 'What are you talking about?'

'*Checkpoint Charlotte.*'

'What about it?'

'It ain't Schrafft's.'

'I hear it's quite colourful.'

'I didn't think you was a swinger.'

Lady Molly's laugh was satin. 'I'm not in the sense you

45

undoubtedly mean. I'm also planning a visit to Harlem and I'm not black.'

'I think I got you pegged. Weren't you on the six o'clock news yesterday with Liz Bancroft?'

'Why yes I was,' said Lady Molly preening. 'That was on the deck of the Queen Elizabeth number two. I'm Lady Molly Burke.'

'I hope you brought a pair of sensible shoes with you. That's one hell of a long protest march tomorrow.'

'Aren't you joining us?'

'Well, you see hon, where Women's Lib is concerned, I guess I fall between two stools.'

'People who fall between two stools are usually left lying there.'

Flo chuckled. 'You're cute. But you see, I got no real kick. I mean I own this cab. Took me ten years but I own it and my cab driver's medallion and that's worth a lot of bread.'

'Do you support your family?'

'Hon, I been a widow for over six years and both my boys are old enough to support themselves once my lawyer gets them sprung.'

'I beg your pardon?'

'Out of the cooler. Jail. A little roughhouse they were mixed up in. You know how kids are today. But let's get back to me. I'm making it in a tough, competitive business. But I'm making it. I didn't go around demanding my rights, I went out and worked for them.'

'Didn't you feel descriminated against as a woman?'

'If I was, I was too busy to take notice. Now I drive this cab when I feel like it. In the morning, the afternoon, not too often at night because it ain't all that safe any more. That's why the wire mesh between you and me.'

There's more separating us than a wire mesh, thought Lady Molly. 'Do you do much private chauffeuring for Sappho Yannopoulos?'

'Only as a favour to Willi Horn. The gal she shacks up

with is an old buddy of mine from way back when she used to be a cop.' Flo told Lady Molly about Belle Grady.

'She sounds fascinating.'

'They don't make 'em any better. Anyway, when Willi phoned and asked if I'd look after you tonight, I said sure why not except how come if you're such a lady I picked you up at such a crummy dump?'

Lady Molly smiled. 'I'm staying in a friend's flat. He's away in South America.'

'Oh yeah?' Anything south of Maryland impressed Flo Hopper. 'Some sort of a politician?'

'No my dear, he's on a hunting expedition.' And I'm saying too much, Lady Molly warned herself. 'Though I must say I don't much relish the bars and locks he has on his windows. I get the feeling I'm developing a prison pallor.'

'Better that then bed sores in a hospital, hon. Them crummy brownstones are always being broken into. You want me to hang around while you're casing Charlie's?'

'If it's not too inconvenient.'

'I'll have to keep the meter running, hon. It'll cost.'

'Supposing I invited you to join me for dinner?'

Flo pondered the invitation for a few seconds and then squinted into the rear-view mirror. 'You sure you ain't no swinger?'

'I assure you my dear,' said Lady Molly with exaggerated dignity, 'I am *not* a womaniser. I'm simply trying to understand this ghetto existence of so many feminists.'

'You sure talk large, hon.' The taxi had left the elevated highway and was now picking its way through the dank, dingy, depressing maze of the lower East Side. 'I'm taking you up on the dinner, hon.'

'I'm delighted. I find you rather refreshing.'

'It's just that if you're all that straight, it ain't no place to go unescorted. It's like walking into a lion's cage with a pea shooter, and I've worked myself into an appetite for some of Charlotte's spare ribs.'

'This Charlotte sounds a fascinating character.'

'You ever seen Popeye the Sailor?'

'Of course I have.'

'You seen Charlotte.'

Lady Molly peered out the windows into a sinister murk and saw abandoned tenements, garbage strewn streets and derelict buildings. 'Where in heaven's name *are* we?'

'We're in the cesspool of New York, hon. The outskirts of Chinatown. The river's a block ahead. That's *Checkpoint Charlotte* over on the right by the street lamp.' Lady Molly discerned what looked like an old warehouse with a single depressing green light hanging over a large metal door. When the cab pulled up, she saw *Checkpoint Charlotte* neatly lettered in purple paint on the door. Lady Molly stepped out of the cab clutching her alligator bag.

'How very eerie. I don't hear any noise from inside.'

'Soundproof.' Flo rolled up her windows, emerged from the cab, locked it, patted a fender affectionately and stuck out her arm. 'Shall we enter, your highness?' Molly chuckled, took her arm and they went in. When Flo pulled open the heavy door, the babble of noise hit Lady Molly's ears like a sudden gust of wind. There were at least a hundred people in the cavernous room, and to Lady Molly's surprise a large proportion seemed to be men. To her right she saw a bar that stretched the length of the place with a blaring juke box at the near end. The bar was jammed and there didn't seem to be an empty table anywhere.

'What quaint decor,' commented Lady Molly. The walls were hung with nets decorated with starfish, barnacles and sea shells. The lighting fixtures were suspended from the ceiling and encased in lobster and crab shells. On the wall to her left she saw shelves supporting numerous model ships. The farthermost wall was completely covered with photographed portraits of female celebrities, in the centre of which was a crude oil painting of Gertrude Stein under which was a square plaque on which was carefully embossed the word 'Mother'.

'I say!' exclaimed Lady Molly, 'what a quaint idea having the bartender dressed as a pirate!' The bartender was indeed dressed as a pirate complete with black patch over left eye and a squawking parrot on right shoulder. 'Heavens! That parrot's a live one!'

'So's the bartender,' informed Flo blandly. 'Her name's Reba.'

'Reba?' Lady Molly examined the bartender again. 'I didn't realize he was a woman.'

'She belongs to Charlotte. They met during the war when they were with the coast guard. Let me see if I can rustle us up a table. Follow me.' Flo led the way to the bar and a caged section adjoining the juke box which held a cash register, a telephone, a stool and Popeye the Sailor. 'Hi Charlie.'

Popeye the Sailor looked up from a ledger, squinted through her right eye in the direction of Flo's voice, moved the corncob pipe in the right corner of her mouth to the left corner of her mouth, pushed back her tattered yachting cap, grinned a seemingly toothless grin and roared 'Well shiver me timbers if it ain't me old matey Flo!' Lady Molly rummaged in her purse, found what she was looking for and fixed a monocle in her left eye. Her head shot forward at Charlotte like a turtle's emerging to ascertain the weather. Charlotte pushed up the sleeves of the tattered sweater she wore and asked gruffly, 'Who you looking at, three eyes?' Lady Molly was speechless. Each of Charlotte's arms was picturesquely tattooed.

Flo put a friendly arm through Lady Molly's. 'A visitor from overseas, Charlie. Lady Molly Burke, ain't you heard of her?'

'Why lower my topsails I sure have.' Charlotte came horn-piping from behind her enclosure, grabbed Lady Molly's free hand and pumped it vigorously. 'How's old blighty, matey?'

'Old blighty's just fine!' piped Lady Molly wondering if she dared attempt to straighten out her fingers once Char-

49

lotte released them.

'How's chances for a table?' asked Flo.

Charlotte hitched up her trousers and nudged Flo in the ribs. 'Let's see what the old mine detector can do about clearin' out some of these lubbers nursin' cokes. Ahoy there Reba!'

Reba hurried to their end of the bar, stood at attention and saluted briskly. 'Oy Oy, Captain!'

'*Ay Ay* you blasted swab.' Charlotte jerked a calloused thumb in the general direction of Lady Molly and Flo. 'Drinks on the house for me mateys.'

The parrot squawked and Reba growled out of the side of her mouth, 'Quiet, Miss Toklas. What'll it be, ladies?'

Lady Molly asked for a dry vodka martini on the rocks and Flo's was a white wine spritzer. Reba began mixing the martini with professional aplomb while singing at the top of her lungs, '*Eight cents a dance ... that's what they pay-y-y me-e-e-ee ...*'

Lady Molly looked confused and whispered to Flo, 'I thought the title of that song was "*Ten Cents A Dance*"'.

'Reba always gives a discount,' said Flo nonchalantly while scanning the room. 'Her favourite movie star used to be Helen Twelvetrees. If she likes you, it's Tentrees.' Still singing in her rich throaty contralto, Reba reached across the counter, handed Lady Molly her drink and then concentrated her energy on the spritzer.

'*Four les-sonsssss ... from Madame Lazongahhhhh!*'

Lady Molly thought Reba was delicious then sipped the martini and with a pleased smack of her lips divided the honours. 'Oh I *am* enjoying this place,' she said to Flo. 'Who are you staring at?'

'I think I see Belle Grady in the back of the room.'

Lady Molly moved forward. 'Where?'

'The far corner on the left.' Flo's expression relaxed into one of recognition. 'It's Belle all right. She's with Tony Mingus, the detective. Come on. I'll introduce you.'

While Belle lit a cigarette, Tony ran a finger around his

shirt collar, tiny beads of perspiration forming like dew-drops on his forehead. 'For crying out loud will you stop fidgeting,' said Belle while extinguishing the match.

'I can't help it,' replied Tony in a weak voice. 'This place gives me the creeps.'

Belle patted his hand. 'Don't be frightened dear. Belle will look after you.'

'I feel like the uninvited guest at a masquerade party.'

Belle studied the face that had launched a thousand jail sentences and chuckled. 'You big puff ball.'

Tony clutched his stein of beer. 'Well they make me nervous.' He glanced furtively over his shoulder and then at Belle. 'I get the feeling they're all about to pounce.'

'Not at you.'

'Who you staring at?'

'Flo Hopper. She's heading this way with something so help me God sporting a monocle.'

Tony turned in his seat as Flo and Lady Molly reached them. 'Hi Flo, what's with the boys?'

'On ice where you put them,' she said without malice. Her boys were guilty, Tony was the law and Flo respected the rules. Tony got to his feet with difficulty as Flo introduced Lady Molly.

'Oh please sit down,' said Lady Molly and Tony gratefully complied. Lady Molly beamed a smile at Belle. 'I'm delighted to meet a friend of Willi Horn's.'

'We're no longer friends,' Belle stated flatly.

Lady Molly shrugged. 'Yesterday's friends are frequently tomorrow's enemies.'

Tony suddenly came to life. 'Say didn't I see you on the early news yesterday?'

'Isn't that marvellous!' exclaimed Lady Molly. 'How awfully kind of you to recognize me.'

Tony caught Belle's mystified look and explained coarsely, 'Another ball buster.'

Lady Molly arched an eyebrow without displacing the monocle. 'On the contrary Mr. Mingus, I prefer my men with their equipment intact.'

'Listen. I'm sorry,' Tony mumbled while Belle wondered if her ears betrayed her. Flo jumped in and explained Lady Molly's association with Sappho Yannopoulos. Belle invited the women to join them for another drink. Tony glowered into his beer while Belle gently nudged him under the table. Flo commandeered two vacant chairs from an adjoining table and Belle thought Tony looked like the Mad Hatter at the tea party.

'Americans are so friendly,' said Lady Molly genially and then asked Belle, 'Are you marching with us tomorrow?'

'I'm a lone wolf, Lady Molly, I don't travel in packs.'

'If it suits you, why not. It does keep one from getting lost in the shuffle.' She removed the monocle and restored it to the alligator bag. 'You've probably heard very little about me, but I'm not one of your militants.'

'That's not the way you sounded with Liz Bancroft,' said Tony.

Lady Molly flicked an imaginary fly from her jacket sleeve. 'I was afraid I was giving the wrong impression. Actually, Mr. Mingus . . .'

'Tony . . .'

'*Thank* you . . . I'm a humanist. It's the ecological significance of the proliferation of minority revolutions that interest me.'

'Don't she talk large?' interjected Flo.

'Oh dear. I keep forgetting I'm not lecturing at the Women's Institute.' Lady Molly was studying the checked table cloth for a simplification of her statement.

Belle came to her rescue. 'She's trying to interpret all the fuss.'

'Exactly,' ejaculated Lady Molly with relief. Tony caught the arm of a passing waiter and indicated another round of drinks. 'I was in Israel last month and spent a week on a kibbutz,' continued Lady Molly. 'The women there enjoy most of the advantages for which women's

52

liberation is striving, yet many of them are dissatisfied and deeply disillusioned. The older women complain their jobs are too strenuous and too boring. The younger women seem more interested in raising families than raising crops.'

'So what's the difference, it's all a matter of sowing seeds,' said Tony with native practicality.

'Well spoken,' commended Lady Molly with a schoolmistress air. 'Of course the Jews have always been more or less a matriarchal society yet in their orthodox synagogues, the women still worship in a segregated section without protest.' She stared almost shyly at her three companions. 'I'm afraid I'm boring you.'

'Not me,' said Tony gruffly, 'I'd like to know what the hell this is all about. You see I'm with the police force ...'

'Yes I know, Flo told me.'

'... Well like tomorrow I gotta keep the peace at this Sappho's protest march. Now when I'm called in to break up a race riot, I know where I'm at. It's black against white, cowboys and Indians.'

'Which are which?' inquired Lady Molly sweetly.

'You got a good point there,' rejoindered Tony swiftly, 'because believe it or not, I don't like hurting nobody. So I just go for the guys what make the first move, you see? But when broads get worked up and start throwing things, you know what I mean? Like I don't like hittin' anybody,' (God forgive him, said Belle to herself), but when you have to start working over a broad you feel like you're shooting dirty pool. What do they want? What are they after? What's it gettin' them in the long run? I mean if I was married, I ain't gonna stay home and wash dishes and argue with the butcher. I ain't made that way. If that's what these broads are after, why don't they marry fags?'

Belle hadn't heard Tony this articulate since the year the Mets won the pennant and exchanged smiles with Flo who was thirsting for her second spritzer and wondering if Charlotte had forgotten their table. Over Flo's head Belle saw an animated collage enter and recognized Pat Drake followed by a delicate young man. Lady Molly questioned aloud the sudden look of displeasure on Belle's face. Belle identified Pat Drake and in a flash the monocle was out of the alligator purse and back in Lady Molly's eye. 'How colourful,' commented Lady Molly blandly, 'she's written me for an interview.'

Belle lifted her glass of scotch. 'She's hard to take without musical accompaniment.'

'Of course,' said Lady Molly, 'she was at Sappho's meeting today. I *thought* I recognized her. She kept asking when could we get together and I kept wondering what she was after. Now I know why she asked and what she wants.' She popped the monocle back into its receptacle, folded her hands and rested her chin on them.

'Hey lady,' said Tony with a note of annoyance, 'I wasn't finished talking.' Lady Molly rewarded him with the enchanting smile. Tony grinned foolishly in return. 'Aw whattahell. You probably get the same damn thing from every guy you talk to.'

'Not at all. Most of them dismiss the situation with a wave of the hand or just shut their eyes in hopes during that small slice of death it will all go away. But it won't. The mute have found their voices at last and for the most part that's very good. Passivity can be a dangerous paralysis. The putrefying sores of our festering society are in need of medication but who's to say the cures can be affected by amateur practitioners? One of our more celebrated British feminists proudly announces that by way of protest she neither shaves her legs or under her arms and refuses to wear deodorants anywhere. Well, my dears. How self-defeating. Who's interested in laying a foul smelling chimpanzee?'

The waiter finally arrived with a second round of drinks and in his wake came Pat Drake and Malcolm. 'Now here's the most fascinating table in the entire place!' exclaimed Pat over her shoulder to Malcolm who was more interested

54

in the waiter. '*Belle* what fun to run into you after all these months! And Lady *Molly* of all people! May we join you? You ... waiter ... two chairs quickly!'

'With or without mayonnaise?' the waiter retorted with practised rudeness.

Pat blithely ignored the remark and looked from Tony to Flo. Belle got the message and introduced them. Two chairs materialized and Pat and Malcolm were wedged between Tony and Flo. Belle pondered suggesting a seance but then erased it as an unnecessary caprice. Flo looked around anxiously for Charlotte but a heavy fog of smoke dimmed the visibility.

Pat leaned across the table to Lady Molly, 'I didn't get a chance to pin you down at Sappho's meeting but *when* can we get together for that interview?'

Lady Molly decided to treat Pat like her dentist, get it over with as quickly as possible. 'Would tomorrow night suit you?' Pat's face fell. 'It doesn't suit you.'

Pat fluttered her hands. 'Oh I *am* on the horns of a dilemma. There's this tiresome creature who *insists* her life is in danger. You know Pauline Potter, Belle?' Belle nodded and caught Tony's eye. He winked. Pat turned to Lady Molly and launched into a full explanation of Pauline Potter. 'And there you have it,' she concluded three minutes later, 'the perils of Pauline. I simply *have* to see her for this series on Women's Lib leaders I'm doing for *Exploit*, you do understand, don't you Lady Molly?'

'Certainly, but I don't understand this Potter person. Sappho's too smart to threaten harm to anyone, especially in her present position. Don't you agree, Belle?'

'I don't know,' said Belle, 'I only met her once and all I ever got from Willi is that she's the hottest thing since Joan of Arc was the toast of the town.'

Lady Molly turned to Pat. 'You say this Potter person has presumably removed some important papers from Sappho's private files?'

Pat paled. 'Did I say that? Perhaps I've said too much.'

55

'You always say too much,' said Malcolm and Tony didn't believe the baritone voice. He looked beyond Malcolm for a ventriloquist.

'Oh you hush up!' said Pat with irritation.

'I'm seeing Pauline tomorrow.' Belle was the centre of attention. 'She phoned me earlier. She's genuinely frightened. I feel sorry for her.' Lady Molly was looking at Belle with new interest. 'After all, how much does anybody really know about Sappho Yannopoulos. Don't a lot of people have a skeleton in the closet they don't want to hear rattled? You've travelled in international circles, Lady Molly, have you ever come across Sappho before?'

'Once or twice, several years ago when she was still with Nikos.' (Nikos, thought Belle, and Lady Molly didn't strike her as one who dropped names at random.) 'I did get around a bit when my late husband was in the foreign service. I believe the first time I met her was shortly after they were married and that was at least twenty years ago. I was a very impressionable young girl then and I found her fascinating.'

'Who was she before she married Yannopoulos?' Belle persisted gently.

'I really can't say,' replied Lady Molly with an enigmatic inflection, 'which is why I suspect I found her so fascinating. Perhaps that's what attracted her to Nikos. You know his reputation for privacy. I was so amazed when she suddenly blossomed forth with her book. Of course now she's an international celebrity and I'm sure Nikos is terribly displeased. But I had an intuitive feeling then she wouldn't be hiding her light under a bushel for long.' She smiled at Belle. 'I was only twenty years off course. But I'm fascinated by the way she's organized her group. It's like a military operation, isn't it Pat?' Pat said nothing. 'She has her aides and her adjutants and that meeting today was I imagined like a briefing from the high command. Take it from one who's been there, her competition isn't this well organized ... or financed.'

'I can see tomorrow ain't gonna be no girl scout march,' expounded Tony wearily.

Charlotte appeared and clapped a heavy hand on Flo's shoulder. 'Okay matey, I got you a table up front.' Flo shot her a look of gratitude.

'What about us?' piped up Pat.

'In a few minutes, sailor. Two of the girls are off to midnight mass uptown in a couple of minutes.' She removed the corncob pipe from her mouth with a benign expression. 'The dikes what pray together stay together. Come on Flo if you want that table.' She did a quick jig and departed.

Lady Molly said to Belle, 'I hope I meet you and Tony again soon. Thank you very much for your hospitality.' Belle assured her they'd meet again. Tony started to get up but Lady Molly stayed him with a gesture of her hand. 'I'll look for you tomorrow Tony.'

'It's a date,' said Tony.

When Lady Molly and Flo were out of earshot, Pat leaned across the table conspiratorially. 'Isn't *she* the cool one. Did you get the way she subtly dropped that "Nikos"? And how much does anybody know about *her*?'

'I know about her,' said Malcolm with aculeate superiority. 'She was in *Time* magazine about a year ago.' He fixed Pat with a Medusa eye. 'Try reading as much as you write.'

'Oh you hush up!'

'I will not. You want to know about her, I'm going to tell you. She's got a list of very impressive credits. She's been on a lot of U.N. fact-finding committees and the reason for the write-up was some *tsimmis* about her effecting an interchange of political prisoners between us and the iron curtain. She gets around. Her husband was picked off during some mission in the Congo.'

'Why Malcolm, I didn't know you were so well informed,' simpered Pat.

'*You're* about as up-to-date as a magazine in a doctor's

57

waiting room,' riposted Malcolm. His hand shot out and grabbed that of a passing waiter. 'If you don't bring me a drink I shall reveal the shame of your birth.' The waiter hastily took Malcolm's and Pat's order and scurried away.

Tony was staring with interest at the entrance where an elderly woman in a wheelchair was being wheeled in by a male nurse. 'I tell you Belle this place is like one of them fancy Italian movies where I don't even understand the subtitles. Who's that being wheeled in?'

Belle elevated herself slightly for a look at the newcomer. 'Search me sweetheart. New girl in town.'

'I wonder,' she heard Pat musing.

'Well she's new to me,' said Belle.

'I'm wondering about this little business between Pauline and Sappho. Of course Pauline is such a masochist her day is ruined without some little persecution. I wonder if her bull of a room mate can tell us anything. She's near the bar dancing with the spade.'

'I think you're wrong,' said Tony when he finally decided which one was Michaela, 'I think they're wrestling.'

Pat was out of her chair. 'I'll be right back.'

Tony turned to Malcolm. 'What about you, kid. You big with Gay Lib?'

'Mr. Mingus, the only time I protest is when I'm offered a second helping.'

Pat reached Michaela and her dancing partner and tapped the black woman's shoulder. 'May I cut in?' she inquired sweetly.

The black woman responded with a look of agony, 'If you're a chiropractor.' Michaela acknowledged Pat with a grunt, released the black woman who staggered backward against the bar and turned weakly to Reba the bartender gasping 'Seltzer.'

'Not so tight!' screeched Pat to Michaela, wondering if her feet would ever touch the ground. 'What's been going on between Pauline and Sappho?'

Flo was studying a preoccupied Lady Molly and said

softly, 'A penny for them.'

'They're not on the market.'

'I think you're someplace back there when Sappho was married to Yannopolous.'

'You're quite wrong my dear. Only those without a future dwell on the past.'

'You'd make a lousy poker player. You had a very peculiar look when Pat was jabbering away about Pauline.'

'Remember, I'm a humanist. My heart goes out to anyone in distress.'

'That takes a lot of heart.'

'It's sizeable enough. Shall we order some food?'

Malcolm was salivating watching Tony and Belle gnawing at their spare ribs. Belle shoved her plate towards him. 'Have one, you look as though you're about to expire.' Malcolm accepted the offer with gratitude.

Tony pointed a flayed bone at Belle. 'Where does that cab driver rate having dinner with a lady?'

'Flo free lances for Sappho. Lady Molly probably didn't want to eat alone. Flo's okay. She'll look after her.'

'I think Lady Molly can look after herself,' said Tony.

'I hope so,' said Belle dipping her fingers into a bowl of lukewarm water. 'Flo's a good gal, but I think she feeds Sappho whatever she can pick up when she's chauffering.'

'I think you're right,' said Tony as Malcolm helped himself to another rib from Belle's plate, 'Sappho's law firm is trying to get Flo's boys sprung.' Belle shrugged and speared a french fried potato. She'd been having private thoughts about Lady Molly and Pauline and Sappho and Nikos and Liz Bancroft and Babe Lustig and wondering if there was some invisible thread weaving them into a tapestry of intrigue. Pauline was definitely in trouble and whether or not an innocent victim, Belle was eagerly looking forward to tomorrow's appointment.

'I wonder why she's really here,' Belle said suddenly.

Tony looked up, startled. 'Who?'

'Lady Molly.'

'What do you mean?'

'I was just wondering.'

'She's making an exhibition of herself,' interjected Malcolm.

'Lady Molly?' asked Tony with increasing bewilderment.

'Pat.' Malcolm gestured with his head. 'Look at the silly bitch.'

At the bar, Michaela with her right hand tightly gripping Pat's slender waist, was carefully balancing the struggling writer overhead. 'Put me down you drunken oaf!' cried Pat. 'Put me down at once! You know I'm afraid of heights!'

Charlotte elbowed her way to Michaela's side. 'Lower that mizzen mast!'

Michaela defended herself with a pout. 'She said I was a weakling.'

'I said you had a weak character!' snapped Pat. 'Put me down! I feel faint! *Malcolm!*'

'She's got to be joking,' said Malcolm turning his back on the lady in distress.

'*Malcolm!*'

The corncob pipe was semaphoring ominously in Charlotte's mouth. 'Drop anchor matey or you'll never set foot in this place again.'

'I say,' said Lady Molly with delight, 'is there always an impromptu cabaret?'

'Only when Mike's around,' said Flo as she dipped a spare rib into a dish of sauce. 'That's Mike Lorimer, Pauline's room mate.'

'Oh? What an amazing show of strength.'

'It's all she's got to show. She's a wild bull when she's drunk. Pauline's suffered many a brutal beating.'

'How dreadful! Why doesn't she leave her?'

'Pauline thrives on brutal beatings. How's your heart?'

Lady Molly stared at Flo as though she was a specimen under glass. 'Flo, you're a fake.'

'If it makes you happy,' said Flo airily.

'That wasn't an insult, merely an observation. You're not one half as tough as you pretend to be, and that goes for the rest of these ladies in residence.'

'Would you like to leave?'

'I most certainly would not. I'd like to meet Miss Lorimer.'

'You're sure *you're* not a swinger?'

Lady Molly removed her napkin from her lap, tossed it on the table, shoved her chair back, got up and headed for Michaela Lorimer. Flo watched the tall retreating soldierly figure with a curious expression.

Lady Molly looked with dismay at the congestion of humanity at the bar. Craning her neck she could see her objective leaning against the bar nursing a bottle of beer.

'Trying to get through, matey?'

Lady Molly looked down into Charlotte's friendly face.

'Yes I am. There's someone I'd like to meet.'

Charlotte winked and said, 'Follow me, me hearty. Let the old skipper steer you through this shoal of dikes.'

Pat returned to the table sobbing uncontrollably. Tony held a modest hand in front of his face as he worked at his teeth with a toothpick. Belle looked hopelessly at Malcolm. Malcolm jammed a cigarette into the end of a holder and directed his mouth at Pat. 'Oh stop crying so hard. You haven't been crowned Miss America.'

Pat looked up and snarled, 'How could you let me suffer such humiliation!'

'She's bigger then I am,' and there was no arguing the observation.

'And you call yourself a man!'

'Now you *know* I don't call myself a man, I call myself Beatrice. Do you want my handkerchief or do you prefer the table cloth?'

Pat snapped open her purse and delicately dabbed her cheeks with a cotton ball. 'Well anyway,' she addressed Belle, 'I know what the stink's all about unless that female Charles Atlas was putting me on.' Belle waited while Pat examined her face in a compact mirror and gave it a fresh application of face powder. 'It's some letter missing from Sappho's files.'

Tony lowered the hand and flipped away the toothpick. 'That's all?' Belle gently stirred her coffee without taking her eyes from Pat.

'What do you mean "That's all"!' Pat snapped the compact shut and dropped it on the table. 'I'd like to get a look at that letter myself if it has Sappho all that worried. I'd give my eye teeth to crack *Life* magazine and let me tell you if that letter's a hot hunk of property it could be my passport to happy *happy* land.'

Malcolm blew a smoke ring past her nose and commented, 'With friends like you who needs enemies?'

'And what's the meaning of *that*?'

'If you're such a good friend of your dippy demagogue and you had that letter, you hand it back to her and say "Here oh divine goddess your secret is safe forever".'

'Well of course that's what I'd *really* do.'

'You'd skewer your mother on a pikestaff if the price was right.' His next reaction was the shock of a sudden cloudburst, but the water was scalding and he shrieked with pain as his chair tipped and he fell over backward to the floor hands clutching his face. As he lay there howling, Belle and Tony rushed to his side while Pat threw the empty coffee cup she'd grabbed from the table on to the floor and rushed for the door.

'My eyes,' moaned Malcolm, 'my eyes.'

And they're his best feature too, thought Belle as she reached for a glass of water and a napkin, made a cold compress and motioned Tony to pry Malcolm's hands loose. She applied the compress to his face making comforting noises. 'Now lie still Malcolm, it was only half a cupful.'

'Oh God,' came his muffled voice from behind the compress, 'I'll be disfigured for life. Gloria Grahame in *The Big Heat*. I'd sue that dizzy bitch but she's so damned

62

broke she hasn't even paid this month's rent.'

It could be my passport to happy happy land.

Belle uprighted the chair while Tony lifted Malcolm on to it. Charlotte appeared holding a jar of ointment. 'Smear some of this on him.' Belle dabbed some ointment on her fingertips and delicately applied it to Malcolm's face.

'Try opening your eyes kid,' said Tony. 'Go on, don't be afraid.' Malcolm fluttered his eyelids delicately and then focused on Tony. With a squeal of delight he exclaimed:

'I can see! I can see!'

'Let me through! Let me through!' Pat was back. She reached Malcolm and knelt at his side with a look of supplication on her face that Belle decided was copied from Saint Bernadette on that momentous occasion in the grotto. 'Forgive me Malcolm. Say you forgive me. I don't know what came over me!'

Malcolm snarled, 'I know what came over *me.*'

Pat sniffled, 'I'll cut off my hand.'

Malcolm folded his arms. 'I'm waiting.'

'What's that awful goo on your face? You look like Marcel Marceau.'

'Oh piss off.'

Pat turned to Belle and Tony. 'You'll *die* when I tell you what *I* just saw. Our very proper Lady Molly just left with Mike Lorimer propped up between her and Flo Hopper! *Well?* Where does *that* grab you!'

IV

Pauline Potter stood in the centre of the living room with her red Japanese kimona hanging from her shoulders. In her right hand she held a carving knife. Her chipmunk teeth chattered with fear as she heard and watched the doorknob rattling. She prayed that either the safety chain would hold or that Michaela would come home and then realized either hope was a chancey proposition at best. The safety chain was attached to warping wood and Michaela would probably be too drunk to function. She clenched the hilt of the knife firmly and marched to the door, pressing her mouth to the crack between door and sash.

'Go away, Babe. Go away or I'll call the police!'

Babe Lustig stood in the dimly lighted hallway watching a roach leading a small detail of followers across the stained, faded peeling wallpaper. She heard Pauline's threat with a defiant sneer and then lowered her head and bellowed at the door like a bull at the sight of a fluttering red cloak.

'Open up! I only want to talk to you!'

'We have nothing to talk about. I didn't take any damned letter. Do you realize what time it is? It's after midnight. I have to get up early to go to work. Go away and stop bothering me!'

'I thought we were friends.' Seductiveness had never been one of Babe's major points and she was trying a fair imitation of Sappho dealing with an over-inquisitive interviewer. 'Didn't I lend you the money when Mike wanted a new chest expander?'

'I paid you back,' whined Pauline, 'now please go away. Mike'll be home and then you'll be sorry!'

Babe flexed her own ample muscles, felt reassured and

pounded the door. 'If you won't let me in then you come out. I want to make a deal with you.'

Pauline licked her dry lips and blinked her eyes. 'What do you mean deal? What kind of deal? Deal for what?' She sounded like an auctioneer knocking down a lot.

'We want what you took. We'll pay you for it. We'll pay you good. You need the money, don't you? You can buy Mike a water bed.'

'But I don't have what you want!'

'You do!'

'I only took my own stuff, I swear!' Pauline kissed the tip of a pinky and held her hand over her head with digit extended. 'I just kissed my pinky, I swear! I only took my own files, my diary and damn it a box of paper clips. I'll slip a dime under the door for the paper clips.'

Babe kicked the door savagely. 'Open up God damn you!'

The door to the apartment across the narrow hall from Pauline's opened and an irate neighbour named Simon Lipholtz came rushing out in undershirt, baggy trousers, bare feet and irritation. All skinny five foot three of him made straight for the mountain of flesh battering away at Pauline's door. He tapped Babe's shoulder. 'If you don't get out of here I'm going to call the police! This is an outrage!'

Babe turned around, raised the palm of her right hand, connected with Mr. Lipholtz's astonished face, and sent him flying backwards into his apartment. She crossed to his door and slammed it shut and then returned to Pauline's door. 'Pauline? Pauline? Do you hear me? Are you in there?'

'Where's to go?' replied Pauline meekly.

'You're a very stupid girl. Very stupid. You have done a very foolish thing. You are making Sappho very unhappy, and I don't like it when Sappho is unhappy. If you return the letter, Sappho will take you back. Wouldn't you like that? Wouldn't you like to come back to us?'

'No! I'm afraid of you! I'm sorry I ever met you! You're all a bunch of big bullies! Go away! I never want to hear from you again as long as I live!'

'That could be a matter of minutes.'

Simon Lipholtz stuck his head out the door and peppered words at Babe like gunshot. 'I called the police ... they're on the way ... you better get out of here quick ...' and slammed the door shut. He leaned against his door grinning from ear to ear as he heard Babe retreating down the hall. Of course Simon Lipholtz hadn't called the police. He never called the police. Not even when Pauline's pathetic cries for help pierced his heart and brain on previous nights when Mike went ape and was at her most violent. It wasn't his affair. He just stuck cotton in his ears, put his head under his pillow and pulled the blanket over both. This city is a jungle in which only cowards survive. And Simon Lipholtz had never aspired to being a hero. Heroes died young and Simon was past sixty, and it had been touch and go getting there. He had every intention of staying.

Pauline ran to the window and parted the curtain an inch. She saw Babe Lustig crossing the street without looking either way for oncoming traffic. And then she saw a taxi pull up in front of her building. She recognized Flo Hopper and began to tremble. Babe's sent for reinforcements. It was prearranged. They're coming to get her.

They're coming to get me!

Mike! My God it's Mike! She saw Flo and a strange woman helping Mike out of the cab. She pushed the curtain back and raised the window. 'Mike! What's the matter with Mike!'

Flo looked up and yelled, 'She's dead drunk. Open the door. We're bringing her up.' The strange woman turned and looked up with a lavish smile and Pauline felt her insides melt. What a lovely smile. What a lovely lady. She doesn't look as though she wants to hurt me. Pauline lowered the window, dropped the knife on a table, scurried to the door, released the safety catch and then stood waiting breathing heavily.

Babe Lustig stood unseen in the dark doorway of the candy store across the street from Pauline's building. She watched Flo and Lady Molly struggling to half-carry, half-walk Mike across the pavement to the building entrance. She was fascinated. Flo, Mike, and *Lady Molly*? But how could this come about? And then she remembered. Willi had arranged for Flo to chauffeur Lady Molly to *Checkpoint Charlotte*. There they found Mike drunk. They bring Mike home. Babe stroked her chin and realized she hadn't shaved in weeks. She waited until the trio had disappeared into the building and then took her own departure.

Michaela was deposited on her bed and lay on her back snoring like a jackhammer attacking pavement. Lady Molly and Flo returned to the living room where Pauline stood looking like mottled marzipan. What a pathetically unattractive creature, thought Lady Molly and then gave the shabby room a cursory examination. 'It's only a hovel,' said Pauline weakly, 'but we call it home.'

'I've lived in worse,' said Lady Molly and introduced herself.

'I don't suppose there's a drink in the joint,' growled Flo as she married a match flame to a cigarette.

Pauline shifted nervously from one foot to the other. 'I'm sorry. It's Mike's Achilles heel. Thank you for bringing her home. I . . . I . . .' her face screwed up as though it had been clamped between a vice, 'but I'm afraid I'm going to cry!'

Flo touched Lady Molly's arm. 'Let's go.'

'In a minute.' Lady Molly crossed to Pauline and took her in her arms. 'There there my dear. Cry your little heart out. I know you're under a terrible strain.'

Pauline moved away and yowled, 'You don't know the half of it!' In three minutes flat she blubbered most of what they already knew about her problem with Sappho and then capped it with Babe Lustig's recent visit and its attendant threat.

'Do you have this letter?' asked Lady Molly smoothly.

'I don't know what I've got!' wailed Pauline. 'I mean sure I read all her correspondence when I was working for her, that was my job! Sure I know the combination to the vault out in the East Hampton House, but I ain't no black-mailer! Sure I took my files when she threw me out like I was a bag of garbage. They're over there in the closet and I've been through them over and over again but I can't find anything that could be incriminating to Sappho. Oh my God how I loved Sappho! She ... she was like a father to me!' She was pressed against the closet door with her back to the others, embracing it as though the files stored within would bring her closer to Sappho once again.

Lady Molly crossed to her and laid a friendly hand on her shoulder. 'Pauline, why don't you go home to your family?'

'I can't,' she gurgled, 'my father won't have me.'

'What about your mother?'

'I never knew my mother.' She howled and then managed to choke out: 'I don't think I ever had one. We were too poor.'

'Come on Lady Molly, let's get out of here,' said Flo impatiently. 'It's late and we've done all we can.'

But *I* haven't, thought Lady Molly, not by a long shot I haven't. 'Will you be all right?' she asked Pauline.

Pauline faced her. 'I don't think I'll ever be all right. I'm doomed ... *doomed.*'

'Oh come now, it's always darkest before the dawn.'

'Please ... *please* ... help me.'

Lady Molly opened her bag, took out a small pad and pencil, scribbled her phone number on a blank page, tore it out and pressed it into Pauline's damp hand. 'Phone me in the morning. We'll all be thinking more rationally after a good night's rest.'

Pauline's shoulders sagged. 'I don't have any sleeping

pills. I can't afford them.'

Lady Molly tweaked her nose. 'Silly little thing you are. I'll look after you tomorrow. I promise.' She turned to Flo. 'What a crowded schedule I have tomorrow. The parade, this little thing, perhaps that Drake woman . . . oh dear oh dear . . . how will I ever get through the day? Come along Flo.'

Pauline scurried after them to the door like an eager geisha. 'Thank you for being so kind. I really thank you. You really don't know how grateful I am. I'm going to call you the first thing in the morning when I get to the office.' They could still hear her babbling away as they descended the stairs with care in the dim light.

Flo said wearily, 'And I think I got troubles. What a sad little mess that kid is. Lady Molly, you're a real good Joe.' Lady Molly shrugged and they emerged into the street.

'If you don't mind, Flo,' Lady Molly said suddenly, 'I think I'd like to walk a bit.'

Flo exploded. '*Walk? Here? This* hour? You suicidal or something? You'll do no such thing. I'm driving you straight home.'

'Flo.' Lady Molly nailed the name to the taxi driver's ear. 'I'm going to walk. I've been in jungles before. I know my way. Shall I pay you now or shall we settle tomorrow?'

Flo fixed her with a stern eye. 'Pay me now please. You may not be in fit condition tomorrow.' When the transaction was concluded, Lady Molly walked briskly away from Flo towards Fourteenth Street. Flo slid behind the wheel of the cab and watched Lady Molly taking long, stiff-kneed strides. Flo started the motor, put the car into gear, and slowly followed. At the corner of Fourteenth and Ninth, she saw Lady Molly break into a brisk sprint and disappear. Flo pressed down on the accelerator and made the corner in time to see Lady Molly entering a taxi. The taxi drove off towards the West Side Highway. Flo followed it.

'Why don't you move out of this dump?' asked Tony

69

through a yawn as he watched Belle clearing up the last of Hurricane Willi's destruction.

'I happen to like it,' said Belle from a kneeling position on the floor as she gingerly felt across the rug for slivers of glass like a human mine detector. With a groan she straightened up. 'This is back breaking work.'

'You could use a good masseur.'

'No thanks. They rub me the wrong way.'

'Hey tiger.' She sat on the floor and looked at him. 'Let me grab you by the hair and take you away from all this.'

'I shouldn't have taken you to Charlotte's. You're still in shock.'

He moved forward in the easy chair. 'I really mean it. I love you. Let's get married.'

'You're out of your cotton picking mind.'

'I know you got problems. So what? I ain't no bargain myself, but I think we can make it if we give it a try.'

Belle was on her feet clutching the paper bag into which she had been depositing broken crockery. She rattled it gently. 'Now try shaking your head. You'll get the same effect.'

'Listen, will you believe me when I tell you I can live with your hang-ups?'

'So can I, but better alone.'

He arose with a sigh. 'Okay, okay. But it's on the record, right? Don't say I never asked you.'

She crossed slowly to him. 'Do me a favour?'

'What?'

'Ask again some time?'

He smiled, took her in his arms and kissed her warmly.

'Now beat it,' she said, 'I have a feeling tomorrow's going to be a very busy day.'

'Jesus Christ,' he groaned, 'think of what it's going to look like when they start burning their bra's. It's like every one of them broads is gonna have two sets of eyes.'

'Here.' She shoved the paper bag at him. 'Drop this down the incinerator on your way out.'

'Tiger, I'd take my hat off to you if I ever wore a hat.'

'Beat it.'

He gently pinched her cheek and left. Belle poured herself a night cap and sat in the window seat staring down into the Stygian street. Somewhere a stray cat howled like an echo from her conscience. Adieu, adieu fond Willi, adieu. Goodbye to a lot of things.

I love you. Let's get married.

She had almost told Tony how girlish she felt by his proposal. Belle still found it hard to believe he had asked. Is he in love or is he just lonely, she wondered. Was he drunk from whisky or the potency of his desire for her. Hey world, she felt like shouting, a real honest to God male proposed marriage to me!

There's hope for the world.

'The little gargoyle must be telling the truth!' Sappho was an incongruous picture as she paced the floor in the peacock negligee, her hair in curlers and a cigarillo clenched between her teeth. 'I now believe she is totally unaware of how dangerous that letter could be to me. Nikos's handwriting is barely decipherable except to those of us who have had years of training. Oh I have indeed been a fool, telling her to make Xerox copies of everything I receive. That I should *ever* admit to being a fool!'

In pyjamas and terrycloth bathrobe sitting on an ottoman, Babe Lustig looked like twelve watermelons pasted together. 'You are no fool, *liebchen*. You are the most clever woman in the world.'

'Hmmm,' hmmm'd Sappho as she stared at the world's cleverest woman in the full length mirror, 'that's what Charlie Chaplin said about Paulette Goddard.'

'You have outwitted Nikos Yannopoulos and five European governments. By even the merest comparison, Pauline Potter is a mosquito. And for mosquitos. . . .' Babe clapped her hands together.

'Please Babe, my head.' Sappho felt the throbbing veins

71

in her temple and wondered if she needed an ice pack.

'I will take care of Pauline.'

'You've been saying that for weeks. Who told you to go see her tonight anyway?'

'It was my own idea. I was feeling so useless. But tomorrow, tomorrow I shall have that letter. I will break into her apartment and *find it*.' Sappho expected her to belch flames but none was forthcoming. Instead, Sappho's face lit up and she snapped her fingers.

'You can break in tomorrow during the parade.'

'No!'

'Why not?'

'I love a parade.'

'Oh you *dumbkopf* there will be many more in the future!'

Babe was standing with fists clenched. 'Tomorrow we symbolize our freedom. I shall be the first to remove my brassiere! I shall set fire to it and. . . .'

'Enough! Enough!' spat Sappho with an impatient wave of a hand. 'At some point tomorrow you will break into Pauline's flat. I presume you have a plan.'

'I know her every move. We will be done with the parade by four o'clock?'

'I should hope to think so. I have an appointment at the hairdresser.'

'It shall be done then. Now what about this Lady Molly Burke?'

'Oh I don't know. I can't think. I've known her for years, she's just an anthropological busybody.'

'Busybodies ferret information.'

Sappho looked at Babe quizzically. 'What are you talking about?'

'After I saw her and Flo with the drunken lummox, I began to think very heavily. Why would a woman like Lady Molly interest herself in someone like Mike?'

'She was doing a good deed. She always does good deeds. She's a crusader. She's always helping the underdog.'

72

'Precisely.' Babe spread her hands and favoured Sappho with a rare smile baring a row of ivory pegs here and there trimmed with gold. 'Pauline is an underdog.'

Sappho crushed the cigarillo into a metal ashtray. Her brows were furrowed and her eyes were blinking rapidly. 'The state Pauline is in, I suppose that flabby mouth of hers has stretched as far as *Checkpoint Charlotte*. You think Lady Molly took Mike home to get to Pauline?'

'I will know better after I have spoken to Flo.' Babe folded her arms and tapped her right foot. 'Is not Nikos kindly disposed to Lady Molly?'

'She's gotten sums of money out of him from time to time. You know how Nikos likes to keep on the good side of all sides. I think the last time he helped her was with Biafra.'

'Biafra?' Babe pondered the name. 'Is that not an Italian dress designer?'

'Go to sleep Babe, you're tired.' Sappho headed for her bed. Babe followed her.

'There is but one threat that Nikos holds over your head.'

'He can hold it there till his hand petrifies. You know well enough he has plenty to fear from *me*. How do they put it here?' She tapped a finger against her cheek. 'Ah yes! A Mexican stand-off.' She snuggled under the bed covers. 'Poor Nikos. Poor poor Nikos. He was like a little puppy dog yapping at my heels twenty years ago. How easily I drew him into the web. It was hard, distasteful work, but I accomplished the job.' Her face hardened. 'And he tried to turn me into a slave. But I am no longer subject to his manumission.' She laughed heartily. 'Now I have my own army of helots, *nein*? It took a long time, a very long time to hold power in my hands again.' She formed her right hand into a claw and then slowly closed the fingers. 'And after this ... who knows? The public will soon grow bored with these protest movements. It won't be too long, mark my words, before protest movements take their place with hula hoops. But I'll get out while I'm still on top. In the words of a very delightful gentleman with whom I once very cautiously and very deliciously dallied in the shadow of the Sphinx, "Always leave them laughing". Now go rest your feet for tomorrow. Your soles will undergo a gruelling hardship from your sabots.'

'First I must call Flo.'

'Let it wait till morning. There's nothing more we can do tonight. Kiss my forehead and try to tip toe out.'

Babe kissed her forehead and whispered, 'And Willi?'

'Pfah! I endured twenty years of Nikos, I can endure a few months of Willi. He always reeked of *ouzo*, she only reeks of stupidity.' She pounded the pillow and turned over on her stomach. 'That maniac Bale strangling poor little Marlene.' She clucked her tongue, shut her eyes, relaxed, and was soon breathing heavily. On tip toe, looking like a Golem fording a mud puddle, Babe left the room.

Flo Hopper's six room clapboard-covered house stood on an empty lot in a derelict Brooklyn backwater near the Williamsburg Bridge. The quonset garage stood in back of the house. Flo was locking it up when she heard the phone ringing in her house. She raced to the kitchen door, unlocked it, kicked the door shut with her foot and made a grab for the wall phone.

'Yeah?' She recognized Babe Lustig's voice. 'I got plenty to tell and for how much?' She heard a barking seal at the other end while reaching out and flicking the light switch. 'You listen to me, large one, I don't have to take any of your lip. I need a lot of bread. I need it for my boys and I'm mortgaged up to my ass. And right now I'm too tired to haggle. It's been a long night. Meet me tomorrow night at the usual spot down by the docks and bring lots of green with you.' She held the phone away from her ear as Babe detonated at the other end. 'Relax large one and I'll whet your appetite. Your Lady Molly moves in mysterious ways.' She stifled a yawn. 'Gotta go now. Mama's lids are getting heavy. See ya tomorrow night.' She hung up and rubbed her hands with a greedy expression on her tired face.

Oh yes indeed our Lady Molly moves in mysterious ways. She was foraging in the refrigerator for the ingredients of a sandwich. Oh yes indeed she is a live one, our Lady Molly. She sat at the kitchen table and piled salami on a slice of rye bread. She sure does spread her bounty in the most unlikely places. Flo lavished mustard on a second slice of rye.

Funny thing is, Flo mused, I've grown quite fond of that broad. Flo took a man-sized bite of sandwich and ruminated like a contented cow. I wonder if she knew she was being followed. I kept a safe distance all the way. There were other hackies on the road. She couldn't have guessed I was one of them. I parked in the shadows of the overpass. She couldn't have seen me leaning over the railing watching her going down that ramp. I'm positive the guy who came down the gangplank to greet her didn't see me either. Even if he did, he probably took me for one of the queers that cruise the Seventy-Ninth Street boat basin at that hour.

Now all I have to find out is who owns a yacht called *Jason*.

V

'Now hear this! Now hear this! Your attention, sisters!
Your undivided attention! Now hear this!'

Sappho was standing on the hood of her grey Rolls Royce
talking into a mechanical loudspeaker. She was facing a
horde of over three thousand women milling about the
intersection of Fifth Avenue and East Seventy Second
Street. Some were tugging at their girdles, others were
adjusting their hot pants at the crotch, a few hundred were
gobbling hot dogs purchased from an industrious vendor
and the cackling remainder sounded as though they were
exchanging recipes.

'Sisters! Please! I want your attention! Will the committee leaders please start lining up their divisions! We
must begin this march promptly at eleven! Sisters!
Please!'

Windows of surrounding apartment houses were raised
and tenants stared at the milling throng of femininity with
mixed emotions. They saw parked police cars, emergency
fire trucks and easily a dozen ambulances. A smattering of
pickpockets were hungrily eyeing the mob. Banners and
placards exhorted equality for women, equal pay for
women, stop victimizing women, sexual liberation for
women and Abolish The Yale Athletic Club.

Sappho's instructions ricocheted about the area like
sniper's bullets. In her black leather pants suit she looked
like an ebony obelisk. Babe Lustig was pacing back and
forth below her with the impatience of a hippopotamus in
rutting season toying anxiously with the zipper of her grey
jump suit. Pat Drake, sat cross-legged on the fender of the
Rolls Royce jotting notes in a stenographic pad. Willi Horn
crouched on the pavement at Pat's feet like a long distance

runner awaiting the opening shot. Committee leaders were briskly lining up their divisions while two policewomen were suspiciously discussing the possible percentage of infiltrated transvestites.

Tony Mingus stood in the doorway of an apartment house growling instructions into a walkie-talkie while one of his subordinates embarrassedly tried to separate two over-emotional police dogs. From Seventy-Second Street to Fortieth Street and Fifth, wooden sawhorses lined the curbs and on trees and lamp posts were posters admonishing 'No Parking'. Several television vans were lined up in the forefront of the mass gathering. Liz Bancroft stood atop one next to a camera testing a hand microphone. Heavy makeup disguised most of the traces of a sleepless night and four aspirins were diligently giving chase to a hangover. Liz's eyes snared Lady Molly Burke briskly emerging from Central Park and striding towards Sappho's point of vantage. Lady Molly wore a sensible tweed suit embraced by an Inverness cape, on her head a smart deerstalker hat, in her right hand a malacca walking cane.

Lady Molly saw Tony and waved. Tony squinted, recognized her and signalled thumbs up.

'*Cut off their balls! Cut off their balls!*'

Tony glowered in the direction of the obscenities and saw Reba the bartender from *Checkpoint Charlotte* with her restless parrot squawking the obscenities with the obnoxious persistence of a television commercial. Charlotte flanked Reba dressed in the full regalia of an admiral, corncob pipe protruding from the centre of her mouth like a vaudeville juggler about to balance a ball. Pat Drake espied Charlotte and Reba and signalled them to join her. They converged at the Rolls Royce along with Lady Molly and all greeted each other like an unexpected reunion of girl guides. Babe assisted Sappho from the hood of the car, Sappho acknowledging Molly and the others with a curt nod which they shared among themselves like pieces of tangerine.

77

Sappho took her place at the head of the marchers, signalled to Babe who brusquely deployed Lady Molly, Willi,
Pat, Charlotte and Reba in a line behind Sappho with Babe
herself at the centre. Sappho raised her hand and then
dropped it like a symphony conductor giving the downbeat,
and the protest march was underway.

Cameras rolled as the television vans began moving. Liz
Bancroft spieled glibly and wittily into her hand microphone. Tony left his post in the apartment building entrance and marched abreast of Sappho. The crowds behind
the wooden guards let up a roar which soon segued into a
mixture of cheers, jeers, jests, gibes and the occasional
threatening gesture, but nobody threw anything. The
heavier set marchers held their banners and placards high
while the rehearsed divisions chanted their slogans like the
war cries of Amazons crossing Scythia to meet the invader.

Newspaper reporters rushed in and out of the line of
marchers clicking their cameras while a brazen street arab
ran alongside Babe tugging at her hip and pleading for a
nickel. Charlotte jigged forward and gave him a well-
placed kick in the pants and the youngster told her what she
could do with herself and Charlotte silently wished she
could. Sappho led her marchers at a measured pace and
with a set expression of dignified determination.

A mile and a half ahead downtown, Belle Brady leaned
out the window of her cramped office overlooking the Forty
Second Street Library. With a pair of high-powered binoculars she scanned the horizon of Fifth Avenue and saw the
orderly march headed in her direction. She could discern
Sappho and the deployment behind her and had to remind
herself this was not the opening number of the Yom Kippur
show at Radio City Music Hall. She could pick out Babe
and Lady Molly and then zeroed in on Willi Horn. Willi
seemed to be chanting her slogan as though taught by rote
and Belle cursed herself for the sudden pang she felt beneath her heart. She abruptly lowered the binoculars and
glanced at her wristwatch. There was still time before the

appointment with Pauline Potter. She looked back out the window down below to the mass of humanity being held in order by the police near the steps of the library. There was another flank of television pick-up trucks, police wagons and ambulances, and Belle wondered at the percentage of absenteeism of office workers. She was so preoccupied gawking, she hadn't heard the door open behind her, and almost cracked her skull on the raised window sill when Pauline in a tiny voice said, 'I guess I'm early.'

'Honey,' said Belle in a low voice as she turned to Pauline, 'never creep up on me like that.'

Pauline's eyes were masked by large dark glasses, but they weren't big enough to obscure the black and blue marks around her left eye.

'What hit you?' asked Belle.

Pauline sank into a chair. 'Mike.'

'If I were you Pauline I'd split from that armoured tank before that armoured tank splits you.'

'That's what Lady Molly said.'

Belle was intrigued and settled behind her desk. She reminded herself Lady Molly and Flo Hopper had carted Michaela out of *Checkpoint Charlotte* the previous night and Lady Molly undoubtedly spotted Pauline as a likely pigeon with the alacrity of a bird dog sniffing out a nide of pheasants.

'I had breakfast with Lady Molly this morning,' said Pauline as though she had won a Pulitzer Prize.

'That's fast work.'

'I phoned her from the drugstore after Mike hit me. She invited me to the place she's staying over on West Fifty-Eighth Street.' Pauline shifted in her seat and removed the dark glasses. Belle felt and quelled a rising nausea. 'She offered me money if I wanted to stay in a hotel.'

'Very generous.'

'She's wonderful!' Pauline sounded like an atonal chanteuse. 'But of course I can't move to a hotel. How would Mike get along without me?'

'Well for one she'd have to buy a punching bag.'

'She couldn't do that. She couldn't afford it. Lady Molly even offered to take my keys and go back to my place and pack my stuff for me and everything. How about that?'

'They don't make them like that anymore.'

'They sure don't. She's a saint. She's coming over after the parade to have a talk with Mike.' Belle reserved comment. 'I didn't go to work today of course, not looking like this I couldn't. Anyway, I have a terribly busy day because I'm supposed to meet with Pat Drake too and help with this series of articles she's doing on Women's Lib and ... and ...' and her voice trailed away.

Belle was tapping a pencil at the edge of the desk. 'When you phoned last night you said you needed my help. Everybody seems to know about this missing letter of Sappho's. What's Sappho so afraid of?'

'It must be something in her deep dark past.' Pauline's voice went shrill. 'Something that must have happened years ago. Honest Belle I didn't steal anything from her. I've never betrayed a confidence in my life. I was with her a year and I've heard and read and saw an awful lot, but honest, I can't figure out what it is that she thinks is so *dangerous*.'

'What do you want me to do?'

'*Protect* me!' She told Belle about Babe's visit the previous night and how even her neighbour threatened to call the police.

'Pauline,' said Belle, 'I don't work as a bodyguard. And even if I did, where would you get the money to pay me?'

'Mike said she'd steal it.'

Belle didn't know whether to laugh or cry. 'Why haven't you told the police about these threats against your life?'

'What could *they* do? It's my word against Sappho and Sappho is *somebody*. I'm nothing.' She seemed to grow smaller as she spoke. 'Besides, I've been giving all this a lot of thought and you know what I think? I think Willi's got that missing letter!' Belle scratched her head. 'Well she could easily have taken it you know. Now that she's taken over from me, she has the same access to everything of Sappho's.'

And probably more, thought Belle. 'I wish I knew what was in that letter.'

'It must be one of those from her husband, you know, Yannopoulos. I opened up some of them because the envelopes were never marked personal or private or anything like that and they always came on those cheap air forms. But you can barely read his handwriting.'

'Weren't they written in some foreign language?'

'They could have been as far as I was concerned. But they were mostly in English. He was educated in England you know.'

'Well Pauline, I've told Tony Mingus all about this.'

'Oh God.'

'He was with me last night when you phoned.'

'Oh God.'

'Stop trembling for crying out loud,' exploded Belle with exasperation, 'it's not as though he's going to put you under protective custody.'

'He mustn't do that, I have too many appointments!'

Belle leaned on the desk and locked eyes with the frightened girl. 'Pauline, are you really as dumb as you sound?' Or are you just a clever little faker, she was tempted to add.

Pauline cleverly sidestepped Belle's question with the agility of a skier slaloming between trees. 'I'll pay you whatever I've got if you'll keep my files.'

'What files?'

'It's in the closet in my apartment. All the stuff I took when I left Sappho. It's in a small carton. I was going to bring it with me except I had to go meet Lady Molly and I didn't want to lug it around with me. If you had it, you could go through it and maybe you could figure out what it is I've got that they want, that is if I've got it. Then I'd tell

81

Sappho and Babe you've got it all and they'd think twice before threatening you because they know you're not afraid of anything.'

Belle found herself wondering what Pauline's reaction would have been to a dead kitten in a freezer.

'Belle are you listening to me?'

Poor Pauline. Poor frightened little chipmunk. Am I listening to you? You whose life has undoubtedly been one drearily protracted monologue that attracts few listeners. Of course I'm listening to you. I feel like the unwilling participant of a psychedelic nightmare. I'm being daubed into a bizarre painting by Hogarth, and it's fascinating me.

'*Belle?*'

'Oh shut up while I think. Pour yourself a cup of coffee.' Belle pointed to an electric coffee pot on a table in the corner of the room.

'Do you have any milk?'

'No I don't have any milk and I don't have any dough-nuts either.'

Pauline obediently went and poured herself a cup of black coffee while Belle slouched in the chair and stared out the open window, hearing the sounds of the crowd outside. Who is Sappho and what was she? On one hand she commands respect and on the other condemned as a self-aggrandising fake. But she's made it big in the public eye and all within the space of a year. She's made a lot of money out of that book, but money can't be all that important if she's still in a position to tap Yannopoulos's till. She prodded her memory until she could hear Lady Molly commenting about Sappho not hiding her light under a bushel for too long. And how subtly curious Lady Molly was about this mysterious letter of Sappho's. Also Pat Drake and God knows who else. And wouldn't Willi bust a gut if I decided to involve myself in this thing.

'You're smiling,' said Pauline warmly while clutching her cup of coffee with both hands, 'What's funny?'

'You wouldn't get the joke if I told you.' She resumed

82

tapping the desk with the pencil. 'There are those who will tell me I am out of my mind, but I'm going to take that stuff off your hands, Pauline.'

Pauline yelped with joy and sloshed coffee over herself. 'Oh Belle you're wonderful. What a relief!' She placed the cup on the desk and jumped to her feet. 'I'll go get it right now. Is that okay?'

'You'll be missing all the fun. Sappho and gang ought to be here in about half an hour.'

'I never want to *see* them again. Please Belle. Can I bring you the carton now?'

Belle was on her feet and circling the desk. 'Actually that's probably a good idea. The sooner it takes the pressure off you the better. You're positively no match for that bunch. How long do you think it'll take?'

'I'll take a taxi and make him wait. I don't care how much it costs. Belle you're the greatest!' Impulsively she leapt up and kissed Belle's chin and then scurried out of the office. Belle wiped her chin with her jacket sleeve as she crossed to the door and shut it. She leaned against the door staring at the window.

Now what the hell have I gotten myself into? Am I doing this to help Pauline or to irritate Sappho and Willi? I'll have to bring Tony in on this. He can sift through the stuff with me. Well Lady Molly will certainly applaud my decision. How *humane* my dear!

Belle had moved to the window. What the hell am I selling myself? The contents of that carton might be completely innocent! Maybe Willi *does* have the missing letter. She's always looking for something to hold over somebody's head. Such as a strangled kitten. Screw it. I'll wait and see what develops and it could be very interesting. She poked her head out the window. Sappho's protestors, she judged, were just passing Sak's. She looked down and was amazed at how the mob of onlookers had swelled in the past fifteen minutes. She hoped Pauline could find a taxi. Pauline. When she left the room I was filled with the same sense of

83

relief I get after flushing a toilet. Pauline. Another victim born to stalk the jungle without talons. Poor Pauline. Poor me. Poor everybody.

The protest march was a magnetic mine field. People converged in the streets from adjoining emporiums and offices. In one department store a dozen clerks abandoned their posts, contemptuous sentries spitting in the face of court martial, while grateful shoplifters strengthened the tendons in their fingers plucking loot like feathers from a chicken. In one establishment that specialized in hair restoration by transplanting, a chagrined technician stared into a recently vacated booth and cried 'One of our hair grafts is missing!' A near-sighted dentist leaning over to drill a hole in a molar was mortified when he realized he was vandalizing the leather backing of his chair. A hawk-faced woman watching the parade suddenly recognized an old friend carrying a banner and yelled, 'Gussie! What are you doing there?'

Gussie, a fat woman in her fifties acknowledged the hawkface and yelled back, 'I'm only a mercenary!'

A scholarly elderly gentleman turned to a bald friend whose pince-nez was quivering with indigation and said, 'Passing before our eyes Hector, are the symptoms of the social disease infecting and destroying our country.'

Hector nodded vigorously and said, 'Indeed Marcus. They wish to cut off our penises and only succeed in circumsizing our egos. Have a life saver.'

'Cut off their balls! Cut off their balls!'

'You mad macaw,' whispered Reba the bartender as she chucked the parrot under his beak and then began bellowing, *'Seventy-two trombo-o-o-ones ...!'*

A construction worker nudged his buddy and pointed at Reba. 'What the hell is *that* supposed to be?'

His buddy replied, 'The Rose of No-Man's Land.'

Liz Bancroft gamely continued commenting into her hand microphone while trying to will away the tiny flock of carrion birds inside her skull picking away at her brain. She

84

took an occasional swig from a thermos bottle filled with tomato juice and Worcestershire sauce. 'In just a few minutes we should be reaching the steps of the Forty-Second Street library where Sappho Yannopoulos is scheduled to make her speech. Dozens of metal garbage bins filled with crackling flames are there forming a circle around the speakers podium, hungrily waiting to consume the thousands of brassieres marked for symbolic immolation. Happily for Sappho and her supporters, the temperature is moderate and winds are minimal.'

Tony Mingus was bathed in perspiration while continuing a steady intercourse into his walkie-talkie. So far the march had been without serious incident but he dreaded what might lie in wait when the ladies shed their undergarments. It was hopeless to contemplate arresting three thousand women for indecent exposure and he wondered what crackpot in City Hall issued the permission to use the library steps. For the past hour he walked with the unspoken fear of some hidden assassin taking a shot at Sappho. Maybe even now someone like that fear-crazed Pauline may be lying in wait on some roof top taking aim and by some sudden deflection hitting Tony instead. Belle claimed he was thick-skinned so maybe he'd survive. He wished it was tomorrow already.

While several miles away briefly in Tony's thoughts, Pauline was nimbly taking the stairs to her apartment while her taxi driver waited below listening to the synergy of his clicking meter and purring engine. Pauline swiftly unlocked the door and entered the apartment and caught her breath when she saw Michaela lying on her back on the floor, bare feet upended rotating a basketball. 'You didn't go to work!' gasped Pauline.

Michaela sat up and the ball rolled slowly to Pauline's feet. 'I couldn't make it. I'm going in late. What are *you* doing home?'

Pauline skirted the squatting figure and opened the closet door. 'I have turned over my problems to Belle Grady.' She stooped and with an effort lifted the carton with both hands and started out.

'Where the hell are you going with the box?' Michaela was on her feet with hands akimbo looking ferocious.

'I'm taking it to Belle's place. She's looking after this stuff from now on. She's taking it off my hands thank God. Now *they* can go after *her* if they dare.'

Michaela caught Pauline's elbow in a tight grip and growled, 'What's between you and Belle Grady?'

'This box,' snapped Pauline.

'You want me to blacken your other eye?'

'You wouldn't hit a girl wearing glasses, would you?'

'You ain't taking that box no place! I know what's going on. Something in there is worth money.'

Pauline jerked herself free. 'I don't want any part of it. My heart can't take it! I haven't slept in weeks. I'm tired of being afraid and bullied and threatened. I've got friends now who are interested in my welfare. Belle and *Lady Molly*, and you should send *her* a thank-you note for bringing you home last night.'

Michaela made a fist. 'I'll give her this for a thank-you note. You put that box back where it belongs!'

'I won't! I won't!' Michaela lumbered towards her and Pauline dodged her menacingly outstretched hands and fled into the hall. She descended the stairs two at a time tripping the hapless Simon Lipholtz as he entered the hallway and she shot past him to the waiting taxi. Simon exercised a long-dormant vocabulary of filthy epithets as the taxi pulled away and then was struck in the back by Michaela as she hurled past him into the street. Lipholtz gurgled a pained '*Guttenyoo!*' while Michaela stood in bare feet waving an angry fist at the departing cab.

Belle Grady was leaning out the office window watching Sappho and listening to her brilliantly declaimed exhortations. She spoke with an impassioned fervour that Belle imagined in the past would have been reserved for a vintage wine. Sappho's vituperative inculcations were delivered

86

with an effective economy of gesture while Belle decided Sappho philosophically fell somewhere between Susan B. Anthony and Jacqueline Susann. She lifted the binoculars to her eyes and watched Willi's reaction and saw the sort of rapture she felt more pertinent to the second coming of Christ. So much for Willi as she searched out and found Babe Lustig. Babe stood with fingers interlaced and head uplifted like a Wagnerian soprano about to burst into song. The binoculars moved again and there was Pat Drake chewing on a cuticle. That was dull and Belle found Lady Molly. Lady Molly was resting on the malacca cane as though she was watching the horses in the fifth race at Ascot. Her deerstalker hat was jauntily cocked over one eye and the Inverness cape now hung about her as though she was a statue about to be unveiled. The expression on her face, thought Belle, was one of incongruous amusement. Belle lowered the binoculars. She heard the hurrying clatter of heels from the corridor behind her. She turned her head as the door burst open and Pauline darted in looking as though the Furies were pursuing her.

'Michaela tried to stop me,' she said between gasps, 'but I made it!' She lurched to the desk and deposited the carton. 'Here it is. Take it. I never want to see it again as long as I live.'

'Go shut the door,' said Belle tersely, 'I want to see the rest of this.' She jerked a thumb at the window. Pauline staggered to the door, shut it and then found the strength to join Belle at the window.

'We women must no longer go through life apologizing for our gender as though it was an unavoidable accident!' Sappho's hands were upraised as though she had hurled a threat at the almighty and was met with gratifying cheers. Pauline blew a raspberry which had all the power and impact of a baby breaking wind. Belle shot her a look of distaste and then raised the binoculars to her eyes. She scanned the mob for a hopeful glimpse of Tony Mingus.

'We must break loose from the shackles of masculine

domination as a nomad abandons the oasis when the well runs dry!'

More cheers and Belle found Tony. Clutching the walkie-talkie as though he wished it was a Molotov cocktail, he crouched below the perimeter of the smoking garbage bins encircling Sappho, coughing and dabbing at his perspiring forehead with a handkerchief. Crouching with him were about a dozen policemen and policewomen tensely gripping their truncheons, alert to any sudden disorder.

Sappho now shouted, 'My book, *The Female Slave* tells you what to do with your husbands!'

'*Cut off their balls! Cut off their balls!*'

Reba angrily cuffed the parrot who nipped her ear while Charlotte clamped her admiral's hat over it and then began choking as she almost swallowed the corncob pipe. Sappho stood unphased under the engulfing wave of laughter and then raised her hands for silence. She swiftly said into the microphone, 'That's one damned smart bird!' The ensuing applause was more than gratifying while Charlotte removed the hat, apologized to the parrot and it and Reba preened.

'The time is now!' boomed Sappho. 'Ladies! Remove your shackles!'

Belle would later swear she heard a mass intake of breath. Tony leapt to his feet as the eager crowd hungrily surged forward. His ears were assaulted by the sonic boom of unzipping zippers and then a thunderous roar came from the mob as breasts emerged like a proliferation of poppies in Flanders Field after a Spring downpour. Sappho stood exposed like a statue under offer by the Museum of Modern Art holding her brassiere aloft as she walked to a bin and deposited the article into the flames. From the crowd came cries of 'Bombs away!' as Babe Lustig revealed two huge appendages that looked like an elephantine case of the mumps. Willi resembled a vertical baker's tray carrying two modest cupcakes. Charlotte resembled a decoration on a ballroom ceiling the morning after New Year's Eve from which two deflated balloons hung limply deflated. Reba's breasts pointed away from each other like sworn enemies loathe to acknowledge each other while Pat Drakes, to Belle's astonishment resembled a sand trap harbouring two lost golf balls. *Sappho's Sisters* made an orderly procession as they dropped their brassieres into the garbage bins chanting their slogans while Liz Bancroft wearily told her hand microphone, 'Our age of protest for the most part appears to be the age of shrivelry.'

Tony's mouth was dry and his lips were parched and he fixed his eyes on Lady Molly Burke who stood placid and immobile watching the bra burning like an instructress at a Cordon Bleu school of cookery. Behind Tony, a dozen homosexuals put their heads together and then linked arms and gaily harmonized in a variety of falsettos, 'Tha-a-a-anks for the Mam-marri-i-i-ies!'

'Okay boys,' said Liz Bancroft in a tired voice to her crew, 'that wraps it up.'

Tony and his police formed a flying wedge for Sappho and company to the Rolls Royce that was inching its way through the crowd. Ambulance attendants were administering first aid to a number of elderly who had fainted and one man was being rushed to Bellevue's intensive care unit. Three teen age boys were being treated for hysteria while two policewomen hustled off an indignant octegenarian who had exposed himself and was demanding equal rights. Several women shouted insults at Sappho as she marched past and she glared at them as though they were expected to fall on samurai swords. In the flush of her excitement, Willi was chattering away incessantly about how glorious it had all been and what a historic moment this was and wouldn't it be awful if some of the girls caught cold. Pat Drake's eyes narrowed into slits as she heard a familiar voice whisper in her ear, 'So much for your sneering at paraffin injections, honey.'

'Oh you hush up!' she hissed at Malcolm. 'You could use them too, and you know where!'

Belle was pouring two cups of coffee for herself and

Pauline. 'They'll *never* be able to show that on television!' insisted Pauline.

'Drink,' said Belle as she thrust a cup into Pauline's birdlike claws. Belle crossed to the carton box which was tied with rope. She studied the box and wondered if it merited a call to the Bomb Disposal unit. It looked innocent enough and she found a jack-knife in a desk drawer, cut the rope and pulled back the carton flaps. 'What a mess.'

'I packed in a hurry,' explained Pauline meekly.

'These are mostly Xerox copies and what's all this scribbling all over them?'

'Little notes and reminders to myself,' said Pauline in a small voice. 'That's mostly why I took those things. You see I was always misplacing my stenographic pad and I would write on whatever was handy.'

'It'll take hours to go through this. How can I face it.'

'I have to face Michaela and that's worse. She was really furious when I ran out with the box.'

Belle lifted the carton and placed it on the top shelf of her closet and locked the door with the key. 'You better go home Pauline. I've got a lot of work to do.'

'Are you going to read it all?'

Belle sat at the desk. 'You can't make an omelette without breaking eggs.'

Pauline placed her cup on the table and reached out and touched Belle's hand. 'I can't tell you how grateful I am. You haven't even told me what this is going to cost.'

Belle moved her hand away. Pauline's hand felt like unscaled fish. 'It's on the house.'

'But I can't let you ...'

'Oh go away Pauline. The next time the Sappho mob gets in touch with you, you let them know I've got the stuff. We'll see what develops.'

'Okay.' Pauline walked slowly to the door and opened it. In the doorway she turned and said, 'I'm going to stop off at my church and light a candle for you.'

Belle groaned inwardly. With Pauline's luck she'll be

scarred by hot dripping tallow. She waved Pauline out and when the door shut Belle sat back with a sigh and slowly whispered, 'What hath God wrought.' The telephone rang and she lifted it to her ear. 'Belle Grady.'

'Tony.'

Belle smiled. 'You sound wrung out.'

'All them miserable tits, Jesus.'

'Where are you?' He named a bar and restaurant in the vicinity. 'I'll be over in a few minutes. I haven't had any lunch.'

'Who's got any appetite?'

'Chew on this.' Belle told him about Pauline and the carton.

'You're asking for trouble, tiger.'

'I prefer to discuss my future over a Bloody Mary. Order me one. I'm on my way.' She hung up. She crossed to the closet, removed the key and popped it into her hand bag. She tested the closet door to make sure it was firmly secure, exhaled and left the office.

Lady Molly was standing talking into a telephone in one of the booths of a row abutting Bryant Park. 'There you are at last!' she said. 'I tried you several times this morning but I gather you went out early.'

'I had the phone turned off,' rasped the voice at the other end.

'Ah! Well ... are you free to chauffeur me this evening, Flo?' She listened with a tiny smile playing on her lips. 'Marvellous. Could you pick me up around eight? I'm dining with an old friend of my husband's. I thought it would amuse him to see *Checkpoint Charlotte's*. Is he what? *Hip*? Ah! Of course! You mean *au fait*. Quite, my dear, quite. This gentleman has been around. See you at eight, my dear!'

Flo hung up and stared at the phone.

This gentleman has been around.

I'll bet he's been around. By boat.

VI

Sappho's grey Rolls Royce glided down Fifth Avenue to her Greenwich Village town house. On the back seat the goddess herself sat luxuriously outstretched between Willi and Babe. The well-practised sombre expression she used when leaving the demonstration had soon given way to un-inhibited exhilaration which infected only Willi. Babe glowered out the window between impatient looks at her wristwatch. As the aristocrat of automobiles passed the Flatiron Building on West Twenty-Third, Babe barked an order to the chauffeur through the speaking tube.

'Why are you getting out at Fourteenth Street?' asked Willi innocently. 'Aren't you going to have any lunch? I could eat a horse!' On the hoof, thought Sappho.

'I have a previous engagement,' Babe told her, each word circled with black crayon.

'Which reminds me,' trilled Sappho to Babe, 'what did Flo have to say for herself this morning?'

Babe's beetle brows were furrowed. 'She was not at home. She is so positive I will keep my appointment with her tonight. I do not like these cloak and dagger meetings of hers. I do not like those docks after dark.'

'You'll have to meet her,' said Sappho flatly. 'Flo is not a fool. Be sure you take enough cash with you.'

Willi looked like a puff adder with inflated cheeks. 'Belle had to be watching from her office. Oh boy I'll bet she was jealous!'

'Is that so important?' Sappho's statement emerged like coffee beans going through a grinder.

Willi's mouth formed a moue. 'I *know* she's real jealous of you. Belle's got ambitions and I know they're not happening fast enough.'

'Patience is a virtue, my dear.' Sappho patted Willi's knee. 'Take it from an old campaigner. Success requires a solid foundation and an infallible blueprint.' She caught Babe's eye and winked. 'Sappho did not materialize overnight like a butterfly from a chrysalis. Sappho is the product of years of cultivation.' Willi envisioned a sea of golden wheat that scythes were loathe to cut. 'Sappho profits now from many years of experience, many years of travail. Sappho has even learned how to realize a profit from failure. But it all takes patience.'

'I'll bet you could become president of the United States!'

'I'm not a citizen.'

'You're *not*?' Willi tugged at her liederhosen. 'Come to think of it, I don't know very much about you at all, do I? Where do you *really* come from?'

'I am my own creation.' It was a statement Baron Frankenstein would have looked upon as slander and yet an *obiter dictum* that defied and challenged closer examination. It was self-confidence that deserved immortalization on a headstone. To Willi, Sappho was Moses suddenly inspired with an eleventh commandment.

The Rolls Royce pulled up at the corner of Fourteenth and Fifth and Babe had the door on her side open before the vehicle braked to a halt. She heaved herself out of the car without a parting word or a backward glance and Sappho signalled the chauffeur to continue.

'She doesn't like me,' said Willi glumly.

'Babe's emotions are exclusive.'

'She gets plenty worked up when you talk about that letter!' Sappho's face was granite. Willi recognized the look but refused to be phased by it. For months she had been bristling with the feeling of being treated like an outsider despite the occasional intimacies with Sappho. Belle had always told her everything, or nearly everything. She knew Belle's life story and Belle knew hers. Whatever else there had been, there had always been a gratifying and

93

comforting give and take, and Willi was naive enough to think this would always be the case with everyone she loved. Of course Sappho was a goddess and by divine right was entitled to the self-imposed isolation of her pedestal, but when Willi first met and was enchanted by Belle, she too was awarded her pedestal though a mere mortal. Willi was determinedly feeling her oats, but oats were tasteless without cream and sugar. She had brooded on this most of the previous night after being exiled to the guest bedroom after dinner. Willi had never been content with residing in peripheries, she was one kid who liked to be right smack there in the middle of things. She reached out and laid a hand on Sappho's. 'Come on Sappho. Tell me. What's it all about? Maybe I can be some help. You may not know it, but I've got a lot more to offer then you've been taking. Belle thought I was a dumb piece of fluff when she first met me, but in time she learned better. Don't you think I don't profit by experience either, let me tell you. I learned an awful lot living with Belle.'

'Then why don't you go back,' said Sappho unkindly.

Willi stiffened and sat upright. 'Do you *want* to be rid of me?'

'I do not wish to be cross-examined!'

So Willi fell back on ploy number fourteen. She curled up like a kitten, opened her eyes wide like Pollyanna the Glad Girl, and gently stroked Sappho's arm like it was ermine. 'Doesn't Sappho *trust* Willi? Doesn't Sappho like to talk things over heart to heart?'

'We are not a suburban couple.' Sappho brusquely pushed Willi's hand away. 'There is something in everyone's past that is best left unearthed.' That's a start, thought Willi gleefully. 'I will not be held to account for a past discretion. Yesterday is dead and it should rest in peace. I will not pay twice for past sins.' *Sins*, thought Willi as her insides churned with expectation. Turn the page, Sappho, turn the page. You're as good as Irving Stone and I can't wait to read the next sentence. 'I'll tell you this and I'll wring your neck if you ever repeat it. What's in that letter is perfectly innocent to the unwary, but were it to fall into the wrong hands. . . .'

Willi emitted a rare rationalization. 'If you hadn't made such a fuss about it with Pauline, then nobody would have known it existed.'

'You nitwit. What the hell do you think is eating me up? Don't you think I know I've fallen into my own trap? And let that be a lesson to you. That's what happens when you don't stop to *think*. I didn't stop to *think*! That rare moment of panic when I didn't stop to *think*!'

'It must be something awful.'

'It certainly is.'

'I mean what's in the letter.'

Sappho turned slowly to Willi and favoured her with a sly Cheshire grin. 'Sometimes you are surprisingly astute my dear. They tell me it even happens with Mongolian idiots. Just remember where your loyalty lies.'

'I'll bet I know somebody who could get that letter back from Pauline,' Willi sing-songed.

'Indeed?'

'Belle.'

'Bale?'

'Bet she could if she wanted to!' *Here we go round the Mulberry Bush.*

'How very amusing. How very amusing indeed. You *do* know where your loyalty lies.' Sappho looked past the chauffeur through the windshield. 'We're home. And good heavens. Look at all the photographers and reporters! It's like the afternoon I married Nikos! Sit up straight, Willi. Look business-like. Do I look all right? Of course I do. I always do.'

Michaela Lorimer steered her motorcycle through the heavy traffic of Eighth Avenue like a guided missile. The meat rack that stretched from Forty-Second Street to Fifti-eth was in plentiful supply even for an afternoon. Occasion-

95

ally the police made a gratuitous show of disinfecting the streets of the brazen black whores who exposed their wares like unoperable goiters, but like General MacArthur, they always came back. Michaela was a familiar figure to the ebony ladies of easy virtue who floated on the market like a shaky currency finding its own level. They recognized her black crash helmet, her black goggles, her tatterdemalion ensemble of reefing-jacket and patched jodphurs and laced boots. She was a vision to be admired by Cocteau from his astral plane.

'Gird your loins girls,' said one whore to three other companions in sin, 'here comes Godzilla.' They were leaning against an all-black plate glass window that camouflaged a pool parlour, looking like ink blots on tar paper, alleviated by four dapples of yellow, purple, orange and red which represented the bizarre wigs they sported.

A second whore watched Michaela with interest as she parked her motorcycle and began chanting throatily, *'My Mau-Mau done tol' me....'*

A third whore started to move away from the group. 'Wham bam no thank you ma'am. I have experienced that one and my Blue Cross has expired. See you in the line-up.' She sauntered away with a lazy gait.

Michaela remained seated on the motorcycle fighting a conscience that told her to report in at the gymnasium giving battle to an adolescent need for the alien sexual release that could only quell her childish feelings of rejection. And Pauline's defiance in escaping with the carton was a psychic bruise badly in need of anointing. Screw the job, she decided, there's plenty more where that came from. She concentrated on the display of goods with the professional eye of a gourmet. I'll get my rocks off and then I'll go home and murder that little bitch. That's what I'll do. I'll murder that little bitch. She slowly dismounted the motorcycle, hitched up her jodphurs, stuck her thumbs in her belt, and mosied over to the whores like a cowboy entering the Last Gasp saloon.

The Black Cat in the orange wig said *sotto voce* to her comrades, 'If I get chosen, just tell my lousy pimp my last thoughts were of him.'

Like the good people of Israel, she was chosen.

Belle and Tony were ambling arm in arm back to her office after a desultory lunch during which Tony hogged the limelight with a vulgar discourse on his battle of the bulge. Once out of the bar-restaurant, the spotlight shifted to Belle and a recap of the Pauline's carton affair. Belle was taking a perverse delight in the expected effect on Sappho and entourage once they were apprised of the news. She foresaw Sappho quaking like a major industry under attack from Ralph Nader.

'Tiger, I think you're a sitting duck in a shooting gallery.'

'You know I don't hold still for anything.'

Tony frightened off a panhandler with a quick flash of his badge. 'I don't like that Sappho bunch any more then you do. I ain't against broads or anybody bellyaching for their rights, I'm just against the way she does it. But you got me interested in one thing, who the hell and what the hell was she before she became Mrs. Yannopoulos. And if she does have a shady past, why did a smart operator like the Greek marry her in the first place?'

'Maybe he married her in the second place,' riposted Belle. 'When you're really in love, you forgive and forget or take a walk. With his kind of bread you can get anything buried. Then when she walks out on him he blows his top because at his age that's probably all he can blow. Yanno-poulos is somewhere in his eighties, anywhere from twenty to thirty years older then she is.'

'When'd you do your research?'

Belle squeezed his arm. 'There are other uses for that public library. I studied some old newspapers on microfilm this morning. It was lean pickings but not too bad for starters. There's nothing about who she was or what she was before she struck gold except that for a year previous to

97

the marriage she travelled with a fast crowd in the South of France.'

Tony mused for a moment and then suggested, 'I could ask Interpol to look into it.'

'Heavens, I'm impressed!'

'Knock it off. One hand helps the other especially these days. That name, Sappho, is it for real?'

'It's for real if you're Greek and write poetry. Nothing about Sappho seems to rhyme. No I don't think she's Greek. I'm no linguist so I can't tell you the origins of that faint accent. Willi said she talks every language except turkey.'

There was a makeshift wooden booth at the corner of Fifth and Forty-First that contained a fey young man beseeching signatures on behalf of Gay Lib. Tony waved a finger at him waggishly and said, 'Now keep your means of support safely zipped!'

'*Thug!*' The fey young man shook his head ferociously and almost lost an earring.

Belle looked at Tony and muttered, 'My hero.'

'Come on, let's go up to your office and sift through that crap. It would help if we knew what we were looking for.'

Perhaps it's the golden fleece, mused Belle.

'You want to catch a movie tonight?' asked Tony with an impish look. 'I'd like to see *Nicholas and Alexandra*.'

'Why, for God's sake?'

'It's got an all-tsar cast.'

'I think I strangled the wrong cat.'

Belle entered her office building with Tony jauntily walking behind her. He was in good spirits again. It seemed to him Belle was beginning to be her old self again, the good buddy he learned to admire and respect when she was a member of the police department. He held a sliver of hope that it was because of him, but he didn't dismiss the notion the true sliver was that needle in the haystack hidden somewhere in a carton box in her office.

In Pauline's apartment, the door between the living room and the bedroom was tightly shut. The bedroom window was open a few inches, enough to fill the room with the din of the motorized traffic on Ninth Avenue. Pauline reclined on the bed with a cold compress on her bruised eye and the telephone pressed to her ear. She was listening to Pat Drake chattering away at the other end. Occasionally Pauline attempted to interrupt, but it was like trying to dam the Atlantic in mid-ocean. Pauline, who had instigated the phone call had managed to explain why she had skipped work that day and why now she could set a definite time to meet Pat if Pat still wanted to talk to her or at her as the case now was, and that first she had some other appointment to clear out of the way which was as far as she got. What with traffic noise and Pat Drake noise and the tightly shut door, Pauline was oblivious to the stealthy activity in the other room.

Babe Lustig was a veteran at crashing barriers. The downstairs door had taken less than thirty seconds of manipulation with an all-purpose skeleton key. Pauline's door had been child's play. Unbeknownst to Babe, there was no safety chain to deal with because Pauline felt secure in her new-found safety. And had the safety chain been in place, Babe would have suspended operations for another twenty-four hours. Babe was light hearted. She was in her element. This wasn't real cloak and dagger but long ago she had learned to accept *ersatz*. This caper would do until the real thing came along. She remembered Pauline had departed Sappho's with a packed carton, and what better place for a carton than in a closet. She went to the closet, opened the door, but saw no carton. She then covered the room with a professional eye. There wasn't any room for a carton, not with all that exercising equipment. She moved cautiously to the bedroom door.

Looking back on that moment it would never cease to amaze her how the door had suddenly swung open without her even mouthing 'Open sesame'. She had been equally amazed to see Pauline staring at her through one eye, the other covered by a damp rag held in place by Pauline's tiny hand. She saw Pauline's quick look of surprise metamorphosing into one of horror and fear. Pauline's mouth started to open to emit the scream geysering in her throat. Neither Babe nor anyone else ever heard it.

Sappho was resting and Willi was restless. She sat in the guest bedroom staring at her half-packed suitcases on the bed. Sappho hadn't changed her mind. As soon as Babe returned, Willi was to be moved to a hotel. Willi didn't want to move to a hotel. Willi didn't like being alone. There had to be a way of proving to Sappho she was worthy of deeper love and confidence and a permanent domicile with the great lady. Some spectacular deed like cutting the Gordian Knot whatever that was (Belle occasionally read aloud to her as she couldn't stand the sight of Willi's lips moving especially when perusing *Action Comics*) or delivering the Message to Garcia or retrieving that letter from Pauline.

That's it!

Willi leapt to her feet. That's what I'll do! I'll go to Pauline and get that letter. Willi was rummaging in her purse. She checked her cash reserve and her nail file as a weapon in case of an emergency. She then left her room quietly as a mouse foraging after midnight, listened at Sappho's door but heard nothing, and then clandestinely stole from the house.

In Belle's office, her desk was piled high with the contents of Pauline's carton. It hadn't looked like much inside the box, but when Tony upended the contents on to the desk top, it suddenly seemed to rise and expand like concentrated vegetable soup in a pot of boiling water. They carefully separated from the rest of the material what they assumed to be Xeroxed copies of Yannopoulos's letters, Belle remembering they came on cheap air mail forms. For the most part the handwriting was hieroglyphics, and Belle wished she knew of a good inexpensive cryptologist.

'This beats hell, tiger,' said Tony with defeat.

Belle clucked her tongue in mock admonishment. 'Has your bloodhound's nose gone dry all of a sudden?' She found a magnifying glass in a desk drawer. 'This can do nothing but help.'

'We'll go blind!'

'I shall go mad. Look, if you're bored with this ploy, go back to the station and I'll check you later.' Tony remonstrated but Belle overrode him. 'I'll work faster and better alone and you could use a nap. You've had a hard day. And besides, they're probably wondering what's become of you back at the precinct.' She fingered the selected Xeroxed copies. 'There's only five of these things and one magnifying glass, and I can't stand anybody breathing over my shoulder. Be a good little bunny and get hopping.'

'Will you stop breaking my balls?'

'That's not my favourite exercise, now beat it. I also need to do some thinking about all this. But listen, be where I can find you. You could be right about one thing. If I'm a sitting duck I need a feathered friend to help me dodge the buckshot.'

Tony stared at her for a moment, shook his head and then said pointedly, 'Lock the door with the key after I go. I'll call you in a couple of hours.'

'If I don't call you first. I promise once I think I've found anything promising, I'll send out a red alert.'

'Okay,' he muttered, 'okay.' She followed him to the door. 'I don't like it. I got a premonition something no good is going to come of all this.'

'Mary of Scotland's very words on the scaffold.'

'Ah eff off,' and he was gone. She locked the door with the key and returned to the desk when the phone rang.

'This is Belle Grady.'

'My dear! I'm so glad I found you!' Belle felt like the Holy Grail.

'Nice of you to call, Lady Molly. I thought you showed admirable stoicism on the library steps today.'

Lady Molly's laughter tinkled like Chinese bells in a breeze. 'Would you believe it never occured to me the ladies would strip to remove their brassieres? I suppose I expected them to be carrying the items in little doggy bags.' There was a pause and then, 'I'm not interrupting you at anything, am I?'

'Not at all. It's a pleasure hearing from you.'

'Well actually, the reason I called is Pauline.'

'What about her?'

'It's the strangest thing. We breakfasted together this morning and she had this brutally bruised eye . . .'

'Yes I know. I've seen Pauline.'

'Of course you have. She told me all about that and I think you're absolutely super to help. You see she phoned me about an hour ago and invited me to visit her. You know I'd promised to have a talk with this Michaela person.'

'Was Michaela there?'

'It never occured to me to ask! I assumed she was, why else phone?'

'Makes sense.'

'Doesn't it?' Belle wondered if Lady Molly's monocle was adjusted over her mouth, she was coming through so clearly.

'Well lickety split down I went, and she wasn't there!'

And why, Belle was tempted to ask, are you telling me all this?

'I rang the downstairs buzzer and then realized the hall door was open. If you ask me, someone's tampered with the lock.'

That takes a practised eye, Lady Molly, and Belle filed it away in her mind.

'I suppose it was a bit brazen of me, but I decided to go up and try her door. Well my dear, it was locked and I pounded away and still no response so I left. I must say I

102

don't relish wild goose chases. I have so little time here, you know.'

And you seem to fritter it away on the most unlikely people. Belle was shifting the Xeroxed copies on the desk, and one of the five was giving her pause to think.

'By the way, would you know if this Willi Horn person lives in the neighbourhood?'

'Of where?'

'*Pauline*. When I was paying my taxi driver and waiting for the change, I could have *sworn* I saw this Horn person rushing away from Pauline's apartment.'

Belle shifted in her seat wondering why her nerve ends were tingling. 'Willi does get around.'

'I just thought I'd mention it in passing. Now how are you coming along with the material?'

'What material?'

'*Pauline's.*'

Belle's tongue was prodding at an inside cheek. 'I haven't gotten around to it yet.'

'If I can be of any assistance, I'd be delighted to help.'

'In what way?'

Lady Molly was staring at a Degas print on the wall of her borrowed apartment. Her eyes dropped to a framed autographed photograph of General Moshe Dayan on the desk at which she sat. 'My late husband and Nikos Yanno-poulos had an occasional correspondence. My poor darling found his handwriting undecipherable and I was called in to help as I was once engaged to a doctor who scrawled love notes like prescriptions and were just as endearing.'

Belle had been mulling a question in her mind and de-cided to dive right in. 'Lady Molly, what's your real in-terest in Sappho?'

'I beg your pardon?'

'I asked what's your real interest in Sappho.'

'I don't think I understand you.'

'I think you do. If there's anything incriminating in the particular letter, you want to see it. Why?'

Lady Molly was berating herself. When will I stop over-estimating myself and underestimating others? 'The truth is, Belle, it's a purely personal matter.'

'An old grudge fight?' Belle was smiling slyly and terribly pleased with herself. The hunch to become foster mother to Pauline's carton was starting to pay off. She was looking forward to the identity of the tender.

'I suppose you might call it that. I wonder, are you free for a drink?' Lady Molly waited while Belle weighed the invitation.

'I'm already booked,' Belle lied. She needed precious time for the letters.

'I'm taking an old friend to *Checkpoint Charlotte's* tonight. Perhaps you'd like to join us. He's a darling man, something of a soldier of fortune.'

'He won't find his kind of skirmish there.'

The chinese bells tinkled briefly. 'He's only in town for a few days en route to the Near East. He's rather an enchanting bloke. He has the most divine yacht. It's moored at the Seventy-Ninth Street boat basin. It would have been lovely if you could have joined us for drinks. I'm expecting him here at seven.'

'He sounds fascinating,' said Belle.

'Oh you'd *adore* Uri. He's quite the ladies' man.'

So's everybody at Charlotte's, thought Belle wishing the conversation would end. 'What time will you be at Charlotte's?'

Lady Molly's voice brightened. 'Flo is coming by for us at eight. The way she drives it shouldn't take more than twenty or thirty minutes to get us there.'

'I'll try to make it but I may not be alone.' She winced inwardly at the thought of Tony's reaction to another evening at Charlotte's.

'Oh *do* try. Perhaps then I can tell you a bit more about Sappho.'

Catnip.

'I'll do my best.'

'I suppose you have those letters scattered all *over* your office.'

'I run a tidy ship, Lady Molly.'

'Yes. Yes I would think you do. *A bientot*!' and she hung up.

Now what was that last crack, wondered Belle. She looked at the five Xeroxed letters and realized there was something about one that set it apart from the others. It apparently had been crumpled up either in a rage or to be thrown with diffidence into a waste basket and then after second thoughts, smoothed out and Xeroxed. The subconscious transmission from mind to hand of a person who kept copies of everything. This was the letter Belle favoured beginning with.

Chloe Waters was severely repremanding herself. What's a good black whore like you doing on the back of a motorcycle like this? Her left hand was wrapped tightly around Michaela's muscular midriff, her right hand serving as a paper weight for her orange wig. Michaela was gunning the motorcycle at seventy down Ninth Avenue weaving precariously thanks to half a dozen beers consumed with Chloe in a bar of dubious reputation on West Forty-Eighth Street.

'Jesus Christ, sodbuster!' shrieked Chloe, 'you're pissed! You'll kill us both!'

Michaela had refused Chloe's offer of hospitality in a flea-ridden hotel that catered exclusively to prostitutes and their clientele. By her fourth beer she had devised a cunningly new sadistic method for punishing Pauline. She'd bring Chloe home with her. Chloe had agreed to accompany Michaela because the twenty dollar fee agreed upon was too good to pass up. Chloe's trade had been falling off alarmingly, possibly due to the current recession, Chloe being an intelligent whore who read the *New York Times* diligently because she also happened to own some shares in Johnson and Johnson. She also feared her pimp would declare her

105

redundant and replace her with a new and more functional machine like in computerized industry. Some of the other girls had taken to calling her Muddy Waters and Chloe wasn't ready to accept the ignominious status of has-been like some faded movie star.

'I'm getting bike-sick!' shrieked Chloe. Michaela hurled a threat over her shoulder. 'I said bike-sick, not dike-sick!' Christ these bulls have short fuses. One thing's for sure, I take a bus back uptown.

Seymour the bartender at *Buster's Bizarre* wondered if Liz Bancroft was an alcoholic. He was watching her in the booth where she sat having difficulties steadying her trembling hands. The double scotch on the rocks he had served her ten minutes earlier rested untasted on the table like a bride on her wedding night wondering if her Benedict was impotent. The impotency was in Liz Bancroft. After Sappho's demonstration, she had permitted herself to be conned into lunch with Pat Drake, an invitation accepted as the lesser evil to spending the next three hours alone while the film of the protest march was edited, her copy written for her and presenting herself at the studio for her appearance on the six o'clock news. She couldn't stand being with herself lately, not since that bastard had given her her walking papers. She cried too much and punished her brain too much with malignant thoughts of retribution. If anything, Pat's mallet of a tongue could numb a brain into insensibility. But it didn't that afternoon. It chattered away about Sappho and Pauline and a letter and Liz's newsprone nose had begun to twitch and began sifting for the kernel that might sprout into a hot item that could grow into a strangler vine to annihilate this Sappho, this fraud, this fake, this creature for whom she had slowly cultivated a disaffection based, if she dared admit it to herself, on scribbling rivalry. Liz wished she had written *The Female Slave* or for that matter *Sexual Politics*, *Sisterhood Is Powerful*, *Scum*, or even *The Cricket On The Hearth*. To

106

author a successful book was like a secret vice to her. At home she had more incompleted chapters than the Daughters Of The American Revolution.

Liz wanted to get her hands on that letter. If it was really of any value, then it would be the impetus to start the latest book she was mulling, a book on Sappho Yannopoulos. It would be a good excuse to take a leave of absence the research would require. It also could be a form of insurance for Sappho's co-operation. Liz was a great believer in insurance. It helped her get to where she was. She had insurance policies for everything including the possible resurrection of Bella Darvi.

So after shaking Pat, she finally reached Pauline at home after Pauline's office told her she was out sick. She hadn't told Pauline why she wanted to see her for fear of a stall, she just cooked up some cockamamie story about getting Pauline's personal point of view on the demonstration for her programme. Pauline sounded as though she was about to swallow the telephone so eager was she to be interviewed.

Bancroft treads where angels fear. Bancroft should have broken her ankles first. Bancroft is in serious trouble. The meeting with Pauline didn't turn out the way she expected it to. What is Bancroft now? A criminal? What does Bancroft do about it? Bancroft can't afford a scandal. Bigger idols have been toppled for lesser offences. Bancroft needs help. Who can she turn to?

She finally managed the glass to her lips and sipped.

'Who?' she said aloud.

'Where?' inquired the startled Seymour.

'What?' cried Liz. And then noticed the time on the wall clock over the bar. 'Oh Christ. It's after five. I'll be late for the programme. Oh Christ!'

Simon Lipholtz was having one hell of an afternoon. While weaving his raffia basket and watching his fifth soap opera in succession, he was wondering if his dreadful neighbours across the hall were call girls in disguise. They were so ugly but there's no acounting for taste. This he knew from experience. But the traffic up and down the stairs. The pounding on the door, the terrible noises from behind the door, the peculiar people he saw each time he opened his door a crack for a look with his one good eye. But what he had just seen topped it all. The big one entering the apartment apparently dead drunk pulling the hand of a black woman with *orange hair*! Then the scream and the terrible commotion he heard and what it took to muster the courage to open the door again and see the black woman come flying out of the apartment and if he didn't know better he'd say she looked pale. And *now* he was hearing somebody *else* screaming and does he dare tempt fate to snoop again? Does he *dare*? He dares.

Simon stealthily twisted the knob and opened the door an inch. He was in time to see a woman with more decorations on her than a Christmas tree slamming shut the door across the hall and rushing off and down the stairs and then he heard a voice shriek, 'Pauline! Pauline! Oh my God! What have I done?'

Simon was also dying to know what she had done but he didn't have the temerity to go across and ask. Instead he shut the door, double locked and then bolted it, and returned to his television set and his basket weaving. Don't get involved, he cautioned himself as he frequently did a dozen times a week, don't get involved because you are a survivor. Only those survive who do not get involved. He involved himself with the television screen.

There was no ducking the shrapnel of Sappho's invective. Babe Lustig looked like an absent-minded Saint Bernard who had gone to a rescue without the keg of brandy around her neck. Sappho had been awakened by Babe from her afternoon's deep slumber and what she heard from Babe's mouth had caused the blood to drain from her face. She had wanted to shout 'No! No! You couldn't have! You couldn't be that stupid!' but she couldn't open her

108

mouth until she remembered to untie her chin strap. Babe had been suffering the verbal hailstorm for five minutes and then breathed a sigh of relief when Sappho finally sank into a chair, with clasped hands hanging between her legs.

'How could you do this to me?'

'I was a victim of fate. I did not know Pauline was in the bedroom. She came upon me by surprise and started to scream, so I grabbed her by the neck and throttled her until she went limp. Then I fled.'

Sappho was slowly regaining control of herself. 'You're sure no one saw you.'

'Positive.' Babe was annoyed at the gnawing in her stomach. Could it be fear? She had never been frightened by anything in her life. And then she remembered with relief. She hadn't had any lunch.

'The letter, Babe. *Mon Dieu! Mon Dieu!* The letter!'

'In the little time I had to search, there was no sign of it.'

Sappho was back on her feet again and pacing. 'If no one saw you, then we're safe. You're sure she's dead?'

Babe shrugged. 'You know I have seen death many times before. She looked dead to me.'

'Pauline looked dead when she was alive. You should have listened for a heartbeat.'

Babe said with a wry expression, 'I could have also made myself some lunch, but I thought it was more prudent to leave.'

Sappho's face twisted ferociously. 'Where could that letter be?'

'I think she has given it to someone for safekeeping.'

'Who?'

'Perhaps Lady Molly. Last night.'

Sappho clutched a bedpost. 'If that is so, Flo Hopper would know. She was there.'

'I suspect that is the basis of her insinuations when I spoke with her last night after you retired.'

'You are probably right. There is nothing we can do until

you meet with Flo. What time will that be?'

'The usual. Nine o'clock. The dock at the foot of the street of *Checkpoint Charlotte*.'

Sappho released the bedpost and crossed to Babe and placed an affectionate hand under her chin. 'Do not look so unhappy. I forgive you. I know it was an unavoidable accident.'

'I'm not unhappy. I'm hungry.'

'You poor darling. You've had no lunch. I forgot. This terrible experience on an empty stomach.' Sappho brightened. 'Which gives me a marvellous idea! Why not dinner tonight at *Checkpoint Charlotte*! It would be so convenient for you, wouldn't it *cara*?'

'You have frequently told me it was wiser not to be seen in a place of such ill repute.'

Sappho ignored the reminder. 'We can all use a bit of gaiety *ce soir*. We'll make up a little party. Pat Drake and perhaps her friend Malcolm. It would of course look better if we had a man with us.'

Babe's beetle brows rose like a hirsute awning. '*Malcolm*?'

'I shall phone Pat immediately and arrange everything! Have something to eat. I want you to help Willi move. I have booked her into a hotel on Fifth Avenue.' As Sappho moved to the telephone, there was a firm knock on the door. 'Who is it?' shouted Sappho.

The door opened and Willi Horn came bouncing in all wreathed in a smile. 'Hiya!'

'Ah Willi! Babe is going to help you move to the hotel!'

Willi folded her arms and leaned against the door. 'Oh no she isn't.'

'Non-sense!' trilled Sappho, 'you can't carry your luggage by yourself.'

'That's right. But don't worry about it. I'm not going anyplace. I'm staying right here.'

Willi's defiance was a new note. Sappho was only mo-

110

mentarily taken aback by the verbal gauntlet thrown at her feet. 'Don't *you* give me any trouble young lady. I have had enough for one day.'

'I know you have. That's why I'm staying here. You need me. I went out while you were taking your nap. There was something I was going to do to prove to you how much you need me.'

'How very thoughtful.' An archer might have just laid a dead stag at Sappho's feet. 'But you are moving to the hotel and that is final.'

'Oh no it's not.'

Babe came lumbering forward. 'You will not speak to Sappho that way.'

Willi unfolded her arms and wagged a finger at the approaching Babe and started talking in her mawkish sing-song, 'You better be careful. I went over to Pauline's to try to get the letter from her.' Sappho staggered slightly. 'I saw what you did....'

VII

Setting aside one item, Belle repacked Pauline's carton and restored it to its position in her office closet. With a cup of black coffee at her elbow and magnifying glass in hand, Belle resumed studying the one letter she was positive held the key that had made it in its own way as important as the Dead Sea Scrolls. The fact that the letter had once been fiercely crumpled did not make her detailed examination any easier, but in the past two hours she had managed to decipher a number of words which were interesting in themselves even out of context. On a sheet of paper Belle had transcribed such nuggets as 'danger', 'pursuit', 'judge-ment', 'revenge' and was now poring over a nine letter word that was causing her severe eyestrain, a slight headache and a touch of dyspepsia. The first letter was unmistakeably 'B'. The second letter was either 'A' or 'O' but the third letter had her completely stumped. It could either be 'R' or 'T' or possibly even 'N'. Likewise the fourth letter might be an 'H' or an 'I' but it washed into the fifth and sixth letters which she was positive were an 'S' and and 'H'. The seventh letter was either 'I' or 'E', but she was happily convinced the remaining two letters were a 'B' and an 'A'. On a fresh sheet of paper she carefully wrote in block letters a series of variations of words and names and after twenty minutes shouted 'Eureka'.

BATHSHEBA.

Bathsheba? As in David And . . .?

Belle shoved the paper aside and rubbed her eyes and then started juggling the four words and proper name in her mind. Ten minutes later she wrote down a likely sentence.

YOU ARE IN DANGER OF THE PURSUIT AND JUDGEMENT OF THE REVENGE SOUGHT BY BATHSHEBA.

Some former lover of Sappho's out to get her? wondered Belle. Why would old Nikos warn his defected wife of anything so trivial? Belle yawned and stretched and decided to give her brain a rest. Belle moved to the window, opened it and stared out at the shabby city. Poor New York. You look like an old girl friend one crosses the street to avoid. She looked at her wristwatch and was surprised to find it was after six o'clock. Why hadn't Tony phoned? Her neck felt stiff and she gently began to massage it as she slowly returned to the desk. Then came a heavy rapping on her door catenated with the jiggling doornob.

'Belle!' The shadow on the frosted glass of the upper half of the door looked female. 'Belle I know you're in there, the light's on! It's Pat Drake! Belle I have something *awful* to tell you!'

Belle unlocked the door and Pat Drake pushed past her into the office as fast as her tight maxiskirt hem would permit her to hobble.

'I would have phoned you but I ran out of slugs,' gasped Pat as she dropped into a chair. Belle shut and relocked the door and wondered if this was the way the lady looked on arising in the morning. Her face was drawn and haggard and the lines around her mouth looked freshly chiselled. Pat Drake was absolutely frantic and words tumbled from her mouth like passengers erupting from a subway car at the height of the rush hour. 'I didn't know whether to call Sappho or the police or my psychiatrist and then I thought of you and decided yes you were the one because you'd tell me what to do because I had this appointment with Pauline and I went down there and almost got knocked on my ass by some positively ghastly looking black woman in an orange wig ... an *orange* wig and it's not even Hallowe'en yet, and I went up the stairs and the door to Pauline's apartment was open and there she was on the floor crumpled in a heap like soiled laundry and that brute of a Michaela standing over Pauline with her fingers clenched like this and my God I think she murdered Pauline because

113

I turned tail and ran I was so frightened of being implicated by just being there because you know what the police are like having been one yourself of course I don't mean it *that* way but you know what I mean and as I ran I caught my heel on those shabby steps and almost fell and . . .'

'Hold it!' Belle stood with her right hand in the air like a traffic cop at a busy intersection, and Pat's mouth was one of the busiest intersections in the city.

'What's wrong?' asked Pat, 'is my hair a mess?'

'Just relax and answer this question. What makes you think Pauline was dead?'

'What I heard Michaela yelling as I ran away!' Pat clutched her chest dramatically and repeated, ' "*Pauline! Pauline! Oh my God! What have I done?*" '

Belle propped herself on the edge of the desk staring down at Pat with a look that questioned Pat's snap deduction. 'Did it ever occur to you Michaela might have just decked Pauline?'

'What with? Boughs of holly?'

'Knocked her out. One punch Lorimer. You know every-time Michaela looks at Pauline she says "You look good enough to beat".'

'Don't be facetious. I'm only telling you what it looked like to me. I mean I only had a *quick* glimpse of Pauline but her head was lying at such a grotesque angle like maybe her neck had been broken. Oh I was so frightened Michaela would turn and see me and . . . you know something? The black thing in the orange wig. That's one of Michaela's kinks, picking up black whores on Eighth Avenue. Oh of course. She probably brought the apparition in the orange wig home with her and Pauline started yelling and Michaela hit her and. . . .'

The phone rang and Belle was grateful for the interruption. Her fingers felt like ten icicles and there was a depression in her stomach for fear that Pat was right. Pauline might be dead. Poor innocent unhappy little Pauline might be dead. Belle cleared her throat and then answered the

114

phone. 'This is Belle Grady.'

'Tony. I got bad news.' Belle's hand was shaking. 'Pauline's been murdered. I'm calling from her place. We had an anonymous tip.'

'How?'

'By phone, you nit!'

'How was she killed!' shouted Belle.

'What are you yellin' at me for? I didn't kill her! It looks like her neck was broken. The coroner's on his way then we'll know for sure.'

'What about Mike?'

'Who?'

'*Mike*. Her room-mate!'

'There was nobody here but the stiff when we got here.' Pat was chewing on a finger nail and leaning forward tensely. Belle was looking grey and worn and possibly on the verge of tears.

'I have a witness that says she was there,' she paused and added significantly, '*possibly* at the time of the murder.'

'You mean you already *knew*?' Tony sounded as incredulous as if she might have told him she was pregnant. Belle told him about Pat Drake. 'Bring her down here. I want to talk to her.'

'Right away.' Belle hung up and jerked a thumb at the door. 'Come on. We're going down to Pauline's.' Pat yelped. 'You're a material witness. That was Tony. He got an anonymous tip Pauline was dead.'

'What about Mike?' asked Pat in a husky voice.

'Gone. Not there. They'll pick her up soon enough. I'm sure she doesn't disguise easily unless she gets into drag and tries to pass herself off as Broderick Crawford.' Pat made a dive for the phone. 'What the hell do you think *you're* doing?'

Pat told her as she attacked the dial. 'Calling my house, see if there are any messages for me. I've been gone for over an hour and I want to let the maid know it'll be at *least* another hour before I get back and maybe Malcolm ...

115

hello Mavis? This is Miss Drake.' While Pat yakked away with her maid Mavis, Belle folded the letter and the two sheets of paper she'd been working with and tucked them into her handbag. She heard Pat say, 'Phone Mrs. Yannopoulos and tell her we'd be delighted to join her for dinner at Charlotte's and then call Malcolm and tell him to drop everything and pick me up at eight. And Mavis, prepare some canapes but lay off the anchovies. Lay out my pink chiffon and open my jewellery box so I can pounce right in and select a brooch.' Her voice went all cosy. 'Would you believe it Mavis? I'm a witness to a *murder*!!' She giggled. '*Yes. Me* of all people. Remember that unattractive little Pauline Potter well ...' Belle grabbed the phone from Pat's hands, slammed it down on the receiver and dragged the protesting woman from her office.

Michaela Lorimer leaned over the rail of the Staten Island Ferry as it moved out of its slip on the New York side and spat into the murky water. Her eyes were red-rimmed and her heart was pounding as though a dozen fists were using it as a punching bag. She couldn't ride the ferry all night but she didn't know where else to go or what else to do. She was in a tight spot and she couldn't think of a brand of grease to help her squeeze out of it. She wasn't used to using her brain but this was an emergency. There was still an alcoholic haze befogging the organ encased in her skull and she needed the sea air to help clear it.

Pauline's dead.

Pauline's dead.

Did I really kill her? I remember holding her and shaking her and cursing her and the nigger bitch was screaming and then I let go of Pauline and she hit the floor like a bag of flour and I started crying and yelling and I haven't cried like that since I was a kid. What should I do? Should I turn myself in? Who can help me? Who can tell me what to do? The fuzz must be out looking for me by now. I'm her room-mate and they'll want to ask me questions. Michaela looked at the sky and the tail light of a jet disappearing into the distance.

They'll make me sit on a stool under a spotlight and hit me with rubber hoses until I confess. Maybe my picture'll be in all the newspapers. She smiled. That thought appealed to her. Then her head began throbbing and she groaned. I need advice. I need a lawyer. I wish Pauline was here so she could tell me what to do. Ah screw, she'd probably tell me to go to Belle Grady.

Belle Grady?

Michaela rubbed the tip of her nose with the palm of a hand and turned Belle Grady over in her mind like a piece of laundry in a spin dryer. Belle Grady? Not a bad idea. I'll think about it over a plate of clams on the half shell when we get to the island. What do I want with Belle Grady? If I didn't murder Pauline, then who did?

She heard an ugly rasping intake of breath and realized it was her own. Sure there was somebody else who could have murdered Pauline. What kind of a shmuck am I? She thwacked her head with the palm of her hand and a commuter sitting a few feet behind her went white at the thought of a collision at sea.

Who else? Lustig. Babe Lustig. Michaela stared at her clenched fists and then slowly opened them.

Babe Lustig.

Willi Horn was unhappy, disillusioned, frightened and trussed up like a Thanksgiving turkey. Her hands were securely bound behind her back and there was hardly any circulation in her feet from the rope that tightly held her ankles together. She couldn't even wet her lips because there was a broad strip of black tape plastered across her mouth. She wished she could rub her chin to ease the throbbing pain where Babe Lustig had struck her with the force of a triphammer pulverizing metal. Compared to the wallop she got from Babe, Belle's punch the previous day was like a feather brushing against silk.

117

Where did I go wrong?

Why didn't I get a chance to finish talking? All I was going to tell Babe and Sappho is that I would be Babe's alibi. I'd say Babe was with me all afternoon playing gin rummy while Sappho took her nap. I only wanted to prove how much Sappho needs me. Willi bristled inwardly. That Sappho is too damned independant. How long do they expect to get away with keeping me trussed up like this? They can't hold me a prisoner forever and Belle told me it's not all that easy to dispose of a body. What made me think of *that*?

They wouldn't dare! They wouldn't *dare*! Why should they kill me? For that matter, why did Babe have to kill Pauline? Sayyyy ... that letter really must be *something*. What kind of a person *is* Sappho *anyway*? Holy mackerel they can't go around doing things like this. Sappho is a *celebrity*. She's big stuff! She could never show her face again if the cops cottoned on to what Babe did and me lying here like this and ... Willi was whimpering. Her eyes began to mist as she conjured in her mind a vision of Belle. How sweet and loving Belle looked. How brave and how understanding, even if the white armour in which she had attired the vision of Belle was a bad fit and clanged when she walked.

Belle! Belle I'm sending you thought waves! Willi shut her eyes tightly and concentrated on Belle. Willi Horn calling Belle Grady. Willi Horn calling Belle Grady. Come in Belle Grady. This is an emergency. Oh God in heaven is this an emergency!

Pat Drake's maid Mavis had promptly phoned Sappho to accept the dinner invitation on Pat's behalf. She also glee-fully explained to Babe who took the call Pat's involvement in the murder of Pauline Potter. Sappho digested the news when it was relayed to her by Babe with the aid of a self-administered stomach massage.

'We must leave at once,' insisted Babe darkly.

118

'Oh don't be ridiculous,' cackled Sappho, 'the table's not booked until nine.'

'The country,' hissed Babe. 'We must leave the country!'

'That's *really* clever.' There was enough iron in Sappho's voice to supply a munitions factory.

'Pauline has told many people I have threatened her. Soon I shall be under suspicion. What then? What do we do then? I will be interrogated by the police!'

'If so, you won't break,' countered Sappho with self-assurance.

'But there's *Willi*!'

'There most certainly is Willi.' Sappho sat at her dressing table buffing her nails. 'There is no denying that. There is nothing so certain as death, taxes and Willi Horn.'

Babe towered over Sappho like the Matterhorn in mid-winter challenging ascent. 'How will we dispose of her?'

'I haven't the vaguest idea.' Sappho might have been struggling with a dinner menu. 'You *would* knock her senseless before she could say another word. Had you left it to me, I'd have led her into believing I was willingly playing into her hands, made her an eager and willing partner in the conspiracy, but no. Not our Babe! You had to heave her out of here like a sack of potatoes and tie her up and dump her in the guest bedroom and God knows how long we can keep her *there*!' She flung the buffer aside and stared up at Babe. Do you suppose it's too late? Should we untie her and apologize and reason with her and give her a large bonus?'

'She is stupid. I do not trust her.'

'She's also besotted with me. I can play on that.'

'It might be too late. She has had time to think.'

'What with?'

'Ach! What an impasse!' Babe clutched her head with both hands.

Sappho got to her feet with a look of resolve. 'It is the only way.' Babe cocked her head and waited. 'I shall make it up with her. I shall promise her a position of power. I will

119

tell her you will be made to suffer for what you have done.'

'You will turn me in to the police?'

'You are so dense!' growled Sappho. 'Suffer for what you did to *Willi*. Oh turn on the radio! Maybe there's something on the news!'

Babe dutifully obeyed and switched on the clock-radio on the table adjacent to Sappho's bed. She twirled the dial impatiently until she found a newscaster. They endured a succession of items in which they had little interest such as an earthquake in Peru, the suicide of an alcoholic Hollywood cowboy star who had ingeniously tied a rope around his neck, attached it to the saddle of his pet horse *Zephyr*, slapped its rump and expired after what appeared to be some ten minutes of being choked and jostled over an Arizona mesa, and Martha Mitchell's deathless suggestion there could be World Peace if world leaders became vegetarians. The next item concerned the murder of Pauline Potter and Sappho hastened to Babe's side near the radio. They listened tensely and the ultimate sentence brought joyful looks to their faces. Michaela Lorimer, Pauline Potter's room-mate, was wanted for questioning.

With clasped hands Sappho's eyes beseeched the ceiling. 'You are good God, oh God you are so good.' She next favoured Babe. 'Come! *Now* I can deal with Willi!'

There was an activity in Pauline and Michaela's apartment it had never known before and it would never know again. In addition to Tony, Belle, Pat Drake and the coroner, there were half a dozen detectives and policemen dusting the place for fingerprints (which Pat thought was a large waste of time as whose would they find other than Pauline and Michaela's), examining the contents of drawers and closets, and in general going through all the motions they'd been trained to go through in a murder case. Pat grimaced with distaste as Pauline's covered body was placed on a litter by two internes and hauled out the door

120

with the coroner walking slowly behind like the lone mourner at the funeral of an aged recluse. Reporters and photographers had departed earlier preceded by the legman for the radio station who phoned his item in in time for it to be used on the programme Sappho and Babe were listening to. Pat had managed to articulate prudently when giving her statement to the police stenographer and Tony silently prayed the search for Michaela Lorimer would be a quick one. Pat couldn't resist asking Tony, 'If her neck was broken, why did you order an autopsy?' Belle told her to mind her own business while Tony flashed Belle a grateful look. A detective entered the apartment from the hall with a look of defeat.

'What did you get?' Tony asked him.

'Well there are two apartments upstairs which is the top floor and both occupants were at their places of business. Both say this Pauline used to get beaten up frequently by her room-mate.'

'Ah, we know that. What about the joker across the hall?'

'Doesn't answer the door which is locked so he's probably at work too.'

Tony looked at Belle and asked, 'What's on your mind, tiger?'

'Meaning what?'

'Come on come on, I know that look. I've seen it a thousand times. What's on your mind?'

'I'll tell you later.'

Pat Drake's head swivelled from one to the other like a spectator at a mass orgy. Common sense told her to offer to make her departure if it was permitted. 'I'd like to go now if it's all right with *you*, Detective Mingus.'

'Why so formal?' asked Tony with a crooked grin.

'Because I'm a nervous wreck and I need to compose myself before my dinner engagement with Sappho Yannopoulos. Besides, I think you two want to talk.'

Tony nodded. 'Go ahead.'

Pat left the chair she was occupying and asked Belle, 'Will I see you later?'

'I think you will,' said Belle. Pat gave her a quick smile and hurried out.

'Okay tiger,' said Tony quickly. 'What?'

Belle told him about Lady Molly's stand-up by Pauline and of the orange-wigged Negro whore.

'When did Lady Molly phone you?'

'Shortly after you left me at the office.'

'What else?'

'Lady Molly thinks she saw Willi Horn leaving this vicinity while she was paying off her cab driver.'

'Yeah? The vicinity or this building.'

'She didn't specify the building.'

'What was Lady Molly doing down here?' Belle repeated as much as she could remember of the phone conversation which was almost all of it.

'Well,' said Tony as he sank on to the lumpy couch, 'Pat didn't see the Lorimer broad actually kill Pauline.'

Yes, thought Belle, and that's in Mike's favour. She reminded Tony, 'There have also been those threats of Sappho's by way of Babe Lustig.'

He nodded. 'Pauline got any family?'

'I only heard about a father.'

'We'll have to put a tracer on him. Or else the city's stuck with the funeral.'

'I'll pay for it.'

Tony leaned back and stared at Belle. 'Since when did you turn sucker?'

'If you can't find her father I'm seeing to it she gets a decent burial,' Belle said sternly. She wanted to add, Pauline had a miserable life and probably only laughed to remind herself she still could and by God she's going to at least get to go out in style. Poor little chipmunk. Poor frightened little chipmunk.

'Okay okay,' said Tony with a frail wave of his hand. 'Get anywhere with those letters?'

122

Belle sat next to him, opened her purse, and on her lap spread out the Xeroxed letter and the sheets of paper on which she had made the notes. Tony studied the papers as Belle explained the little she had accomplished. '*Bathsheba?*' wheezed Tony.

The men in the room turned to look at Tony while Belle's fingernail underlined the test sentence she had devised: '*You are in danger of the pursuit and judgement of the revenge sought by Bathsheba.*'

'Not bad,' said Tony, 'you got a nice style.'

A detective interrupted. 'We've covered the place, Tony. What next?'

'Back to the precinct,' ordered Tony, 'and get it all checked out by forensics. Goldberg ... You and Kelly go up to the meat rack on Eighth and find us a black whore in an orange wig who might have been a witness to the killing.'

Goldberg exchanged glances with Kelly who was shuddering, and said to Tony, 'There's an awful lot of them.'

'Go on up there!' shouted Tony. He turned to Belle, 'What about Lady Molly? Do I bring her in?'

Belle turned the suggestion over in her mind and then said, 'No, not yet. She's asked me to join her at Charlotte's for dinner with some friend. Let me handle her for the time being.'

'You ain't on the force any longer, tiger.'

'Pauline was my client.' She indicated the letter on her lap. 'I'm holding the hot potato.'

Tony scratched his chin. 'How many people know you got this thing?'

Belle favoured him with a gallic shrug. 'Who's to know? Pat and Lady Molly for sure ... oh yes, and Michaela ... but as to anybody else your guess is as good as mine. Maybe Sappho and Babe Lustig.'

'*Her* we bring in.'

'Later.'

'What's with later?' Tony's voice had risen several

octaves. 'I got a murder case here. I want to break it and I want to break it fast!'

Belle patted his hand. 'Haste makes waste.'

'Don't quote me from samplers. You know the pressure we're under.'

'I know the pressure you're under but I also know Sappho and Babe are going to be at Charlotte's later. Will you trust me with this for a few more hours? You got most of your suspects under one roof. Just spot a couple of boys near the place from nine o'clock onward. You can either have them tailed from there or bring them in. Better yet you should be with me.'

Tony went white and then resigned himself to his fate. 'Whattahell, I suppose if I go there often enough I can build up an immunity. What are you looking at?'

Belle's eyes had been trained through the open door of the murder apartment at the neighbouring door across the hall. She was positive she had seen that door open a crack and then just as quickly shut again. She whispered the information to Tony. Tony dismissed the other detectives and lit a cigarette.

'Let me handle this one,' offered Belle.

'Be my guest.'

Belle strolled casually to Simon Lipholtz's door. The square of cardboard under the bell told her the occupant's name was Simon Lipholtz. She pressed the bell and waited. She pressed the bell again and then tapped gently on the door. She called out Lipholtz's name. The frightened old man sat tensely holding the raffia basket wondering if there was any point in putting it over his head. He heard Belle say through the door, 'Mr. Lipholtz, we know you're in there.' Her voice was sweet and friendly. 'We simply wish to ask you a few questions. Please cooperate with us, Mr. Lipholtz. It's such an unnecessary bother to issue a warrant for your arrest.' Lipholtz bit his lip. 'It's everyone's duty to be a good citizen and cooperate with the police.'

Tony was framed in Pauline's doorway watching and

listening to Belle with admiration. Lipholtz was opening his door. Lipholtz poked his head out and Tony saw a bald turtle with a Charlie Chaplin moustache and heard familiar lyrics, 'I don't want to get involved.' Belle had expected him to say 'I already gave at the office.'

She mustered her most winning smile. 'We do need your help, Mister Lipholtz. Shall I come inside or would you like to come into your neighbour's apartment?' Lipholtz recoiled and made a move to shut the door, but Belle's foot was firmly wedged against it. 'Don't be afraid, Mister Lipholtz. Did you know Pauline Potter?' He nodded in three nervous jerks. 'She was murdered a few hours ago.'

'Please lady,' said Lipholtz with a whimpering voice, 'I'm an old man. I don't see so good and I don't hear so good.'

'You were home all day?' asked Belle swiftly.

'I'm always home ... that is ...'

'Please Mr. Lipholtz. Please tell us anything you might have heard or seen. Anything that you think might help us.' She might have been dealing with a shy child on its first day at school. 'We know Miss Potter had some visitors today. Perhaps you happened to see some of them. After all, we're all curious aren't we? Sometimes you open your door a little when you hear something strange. You were a good neighbour last night weren't you when the big woman was trying to get into Miss Potter's apartment.' Lipholtz was blinking his eyes rapidly and wondering if this lady was some kind of sorceress. 'I'm a friend . . . or was a friend of Miss Potter's. She told me all about it. She was so very grateful. Come on Mister Lipholtz. Let's sit down and have a little chat. It won't take long.'

'You promise? I don't want to miss *All In The Family*.'

'I promise. You won't miss one precious moment. I haven't introduced myself, have I? Well my name is Belle Grady and ...'

And that was the last Tony heard. Belle was inside Simon Lipholtz's apartment with the door shut.

'Eeeeeeeeeyyyyyyy – *ouch*!'

Sappho had torn the tape free from Willi Horn's mouth and clucked sympathetically at the crimson broiled state of Willi's upper lip. Tiny blonde uprooted hairs clung to the adhesive and Sappho gingerly dropped the tape into a wastepaper basket which was a bit of a bother as the adhesive insisted on clinging to her fingers. Babe was stolidly untying Willi's wrists and ankles while Sappho gently stroked their victim's cheek and cooed, 'I shall never forgive myself for this. I have misjudged my poor little precious.' She lifted Willi into her arms and held her tightly while gently patting her back and gently praying to herself the action wouldn't result in a burp. 'Babe didn't give you a chance to explain yourself, did she?'

'Noooooo!' wailed Willi.

'Babe is so pigheaded. She is so impetuous.'

'She's a big fat tub of lard!' howled Willi.

Babe considered breaking her ankles but reason prevailed.

'Now now my precious loyal darling,' soothed Sappho, 'but you sounded so threatening ...'

Willi pulled away from her and began rubbing her aching wrists. 'You didn't give me a chance to finish. Nobody ever gives me a chance to finish. I was just going to say I'd be Babe's alibi, that's all!'

'We should have realized that, shouldn't we Babe?' Babe was glowering. Sappho diligently applied herself to massaging one of Willi's ankles. 'Shall we tell you what we just heard on the radio?'

Willi was playing her big moment for all it was worth and simply pouted and hung her head and wriggled her toes and was gratified to see they could function.

'We heard something wonderful on the radio, Willi.'

'What?'

'The police are looking for Michaela Lorimer. *She* killed Pauline.'

Willi's head shot up. 'She didn't!'

126

'She *did*. We just heard it on the radio and realized what a terrible injustice we've inflicted upon you because *liebchen*, you sounded like you were trying to *blackmail* us.'

Willi said in a soggy voice, 'That wasn't what it was meant to sound like.' She sniffled and then continued. '*Michaela* killed Pauline?' Babe nodded solemnly. 'Then what did I see *you* doing?'

'I was searching for the letter,' replied Babe piously.

'You were shaking the hell out of her!' blared Willi. She turned to Sappho. 'I heard Pauline gurgle and start to sag and I got so frightened I ran up the stairs to hide until Babe went away. When I heard Babe go, I ran back down and looked into Pauline's apartment and she was laying on the floor face down with her hands and legs outstretched and ugh what an awful sight. I was so nauseous I had to stop at Chock Full Of Nuts for a malted . . .'

Sappho tenderly laced fingers with Willi. 'Do you still love Sappho?' After a nervous moment, Willi jerked her head up and down and Sappho smiled coyly. 'You forgive us?' Another nervous moment and Willi repeated the puppet-like movement of her head. 'Now I have a surprise for you.'

'What!'

'We're going to go away on a *long* vacation!'

'You mean East Hampton?' Willi's voice was listless. Sappho's rented Long Island estate bored her.

'Farrrrr away.'

'Where? Where?' Willi was bouncing up and down as though she was about to be spoon fed chocolate pudding.

'South America!'

'Wow!'

'South America!' Sappho chucked Willi under the chin. '*Brazil!*'

'Beautiful!'

'Sappho is exhausted. She needs a rest. I have friends there who have been imploring me to visit them for months. And I know they will adore *you*. Are you excited?'

'*Excited!*' Willi was punching the air with a fist. 'Sappho baby I'm hanging right in there with you!' Sappho unconsciously put a hand to her throat.

'Forgive and forget?'

'Forgiven and forgotten! Wheeee!' Willie leapt from the bed and pirouetted around the room while Sappho shot a quick wink at Babe who held a stranglehold on a pillow, privately wishing it was Willi's throat.

Sappho was on her feet poised on one leg like a tightrope walker who'd death-defy anything so long as the safety net was securely in place beneath her. 'Calm down, Willi, calm down. Have a bath and put on your prettiest hot pants. We're having a little party tonight at *Checkpoint Charlotte.*'

'I shall drink champagne from your slipper!' simpered Willi.

Babe grimaced while Sappho advised Willi she was planning to wear her mink-lined boots and for mink champagne was a no no. 'Come Babe, we must call the travel agent and settle the arrangements for tomorrow.'

'Tomorrow?' questioned Babe and then her face settled into a small smile. 'Yes tomorrow is a good idea.' Tonight would be even better, Babe was thinking, but Sappho knew best. Sappho always knew best. She always chose the right moment for an exit.

When Belle returned to Pauline's apartment after fifteen minutes with Simon Lipholtz, she gently closed the door behind her and made an exaggerated gesture of wiping imaginary perspiration from her brow. 'He makes the F.B.I. look like amateurs.'

'Come on tiger, give,' prodded Tony anxiously.

'Well in the first place he corroborates Pat's statement. The prostie in the orange wig and Michaela standing over the body yelling "What have I done" etcetera. But to begin at the beginning let me tell you Simon Lipholtz has had a very busy day. The first person he saw sounds like Babe

128

Lustig. He only had a fast glimpse but he's pretty sure it's the same woman he threatened with the police last night. Seeing her was purely by accident. He was going downstairs to empty his garbage pail. Anyway, he darted back into the apartment when he saw Babe leaving this one with the door slightly ajar. Simon couldn't see in and after waiting a few minutes was planning to take a look when he saw a woman come down from the upstairs landing. So he shot back into his apartment again. His description of her is a little sketchy but for me it fits Willi.'

Tony was making notes rapidly while Belle continued recapping what she gleaned from Simon Lipholtz which she had accepted from the old man with verisimilitude. 'Well after he heard Willi leaving, he gave it a few minutes and then started out again with the garbage.'

'Thank God he's a determined man,' said Tony wryly.

'Amen,' countered Belle. 'Anyway, that sortie was also doomed to failure. Up the stairs was coming the one and only never to be forgotten and needs no introduction Lady Molly.'

'Better late then never.'

'Indeed. At this point Simon did notice Pauline's door was shut which leads me to believe Willi poked her head in and then right out again shutting the door when she left.'

'So Lady Molly is next banging on the door.'

'That's right. And to my knowledge she's the one with the legitimate reason for being here having been invited by the victim herself.' The victim. No longer 'Pauline'. The victim. Belle rubbed her damp palms together. 'It was after presumably receiving no response from ... from Pauline that Lady Molly went all the way back home and phoned me.'

'Right.'

'Also wrong.' Tony look up questioningly. 'Lady Molly wasn't alone. There was a man with her.'

VIII

'A man?' said Tony with delight. Belle thought she heard him salivating.

'A man. Very sketchy description for the simple reason Simon never caught a good look at his face. Once they were at the door he did brave another quick peek but their backs were to him. The best he could give me was that the party was taller then Lady Molly which puts him anywhere between five ten and six anything and was slim but looked solid.'

'How long did they hang around?'

'He couldn't say because he had a phone call from a niece and that occupied maybe five minutes. Anyway, still nursing his ambition to be rid of his garbage, he made for the door again. Brace yourself.'

'He saw Mayor Lindsay.'

'Your radar's working but slightly off. He recognized Liz Bancroft.' Belle wondered if there was a tea kettle on the stove and then realized it was Tony who was whistling.

'Now what the hell would *she* be doing here?'

'Ask her. But my money is on this precious little letter.' She waved her handbag where the hot item now reposed again. 'There's something I forgot to tell you. After my case of justifiable homicide yesterday, I was solacing myself with a drink at some new bar on Bleecker Street. Apparently Liz lives in the area, saw me through the window and joined me for a drink. She was a bit tanked up to begin with and went into a long spiel on how much she's grown to dislike Willi and by inference Sappho and what else can I tell you? Like anybody else you can name she knows about the letter and maybe she was trying to get her hands on it.' Belle withdrew into a strange silence.

'Okay, tiger,' said Tony after sixty seconds, 'what's on your mind? That look's back on your face again.'

'Just entertaining some crazy little thought that's been nibbling at my brain.'

Tony went to her and put an arm around her shoulder. 'Be a real pal. Go halfies with me.'

'Sport, is it perhaps possible Pauline was already dead when Michaela came home with the dinge?'

'At the moment feeling very dispirited and lazy, I say I hope not. But knowing in this rotten business anything is possible, I admit it could be. But what about "Oh my God what have I done"?'

Belle began walking slowly in a circle. 'Well from what I've been told about her by Pauline, a couple of drinks and she's not sure what planet she's on. You saw that black eye of Pauline's. She got the decoration from Michaela this morning. Then Michaela went for her again when Pauline came to get the carton of papers. Of course for once we are grateful Pauline managed to outdistance our Michaela.'

'So them words Pat Drake and Lipholtz heard could be remorse, right?'

'Could be. I hear science has perfected a robot that shows emotions.'

'Oh boy oh boy oh boy oh boy. So if the room-mate didn't do it, we start with the Lustig broad and work our way up.' An elfin grin played on his mouth. 'Who's your first choice?'

'Oh Christ. I suppose Lustig. She's the most obvious. We know her credentials.'

'Maybe Willi?' The elfin grin had spread. 'She could have some private motive in getting that letter.'

'Stop looking so smart ass. This doesn't look like any case of premeditated murder. Willi doesn't have the brain to plan a killing. It takes a lot of thought and for Willi thinking hurts. The height of her intellect is to quote Judith Crist.'

'Accidental homicide doesn't require any thinking.'

131

'It takes a lot of strength to break a neck! Willi suffers when she peels an orange!'

'Boy do you broads stick together!'

'We have to, we're all we've got!'

'Stop yelling or Lipholtz'll take a dive out of his window!'

'Then he'll finally get rid of his garbage!'

'Calm down tiger, calm down. I got to get going on this list of possible suspects.'

'I told you how to save time. Most of them will be converging on Charlotte's place in another hour, though I can't vouch for Liz.' Belle sank on to the couch with a sulking expression.

'Give us a smile tiger and I'll let you in on a little secret.'

Belle flashed a quick phony smile and then went glum again.

'Pauline's neck break was a superficial fracture of the verterbrae.'

'Not enough to kill her?'

'Only enough to give her a stiff neck from a correctional brace. That's why the autopsy. You want to know what the coroner thinks?' Belle's look told him she was all ears. 'He thinks she died of a heart attack.'

'Are you pulling my leg?'

'Any time you like but not now. He thinks she died of fright. Fear accumulates, you know. It builds up in the system until it gets triggered by some sudden anything and whammo, there goes the old ticker.'

'So it's murder by indirection.'

'That's what it sounds like tiger. Now who on this list frightened that kid to death?'

Belle jumped to her feet. 'Are you buying me a drink before dinner or do you want to go back to the precinct?'

'I'll phone them and tell them where I'll be. In fact I'll kill two birds and have them track down Bancroft. But I'm leaving you the minute Goldberg and Kelly pick up the spook.'

Belle couldn't resist her next remark. 'By now she could have switched wigs, you know.'

'Gee but you're a joy and comfort to me in my old age.' He sat at the phone and dialled and watched Belle lovingly as she took a compact from her handbag and began repairing her face. Whoever this Bathsheba is, thought Tony, she don't hold no candle to Belle I'll bet.

Belle was wondering who made the anonymous phone call reporting Pauline's death.

Lady Molly sat relaxed in the back seat of Flo Potter's taxicab platonically holding hands with her handsome escort. Uri Bar Ishiba was an impressive looking man who looked a decade younger than his fifty years. His strong face was deeply tanned and adorned by a topiary beard. His good crop of black hair was heavily peppered with grey and when he smiled, his cheeks dimpled boyishly and as for his teeth, thought Flo as she sneaked an occasional glance at him in the rear-view mirror, they were welcome to bite into her any time he elected. From the moment she set eyes on him when he led Lady Molly down the brownstone stairs, Flo stamped the look of him with the Hopper Seal Of Approval. Flo always had a preference for large men, and here was one she could heartily adapt to suit her every sexual fantasy.

'My turn to say a penny for them, Flo.'

'Huh? Oh ... just thinking about poor Pauline Potter,' she lied.

'Absolutely tragic, the poor little thing.' Lady Molly responded in kind when Uri gently squeezed her hand. She told Flo about the appointment Pauline never kept.

'Wouldn't it be awful if she was already dead behind that door while you were pounding it?' Flo was almost drooling.

'I have considered that. Indeed I have considered that.'

'Well the cops'll catch up with Mike. I always had a feeling one of those punches of hers would be fatal. Well, Pauline's well out of it. She didn't fit in no place.'

'Flo, how heartless!'

Flo responded with a rude noise. 'Ah the world's over-populated with unnecessary people. You read the papers. We're overcrowded. What joker said the weak shall inherit the earth?'

'The meek,' corrected Lady Molly.

'Same thing,' rasped Flo. 'They ain't gonna inherit nothing because they don't survive to get it.'

'You of course are a survivor.' It was Uri who spoke and Flo found his dulcetly accented voice overpoweringly sexy and had to tighten her grip on the steering wheel.

'You bet your sweet bippy. When my time comes, they'll have to hammer me into my grave. I'll tell you what I'd like to know. I'd like to know who's got their hands on that letter of Sappho's Pauline had stashed away.'

'Belle Grady has it,' said Lady Molly as though she thought everybody knew.

Flo was agog. 'How'd you find *that* out?' Lady Molly told her. 'I wonder if Sappho knows,' said Flo mysteriously. If she doesn't, thought Lady Molly with a sagacious expression on her face, she soon will.

'Are we almost there?' Uri asked Lady Molly. 'This neighbourhood looks so sinister.'

Lady Molly smiled. 'We're almost there, Uri darling. We're quite safe with Flo, aren't we Flo?'

'Your boy friend looks as though he can take care of himself.' Looks might be deceiving, Flo reminded herself, but she recognized a ringer then she saw one. This one's got muscle he hasn't even used yet. And then she found herself wondering, could this be the man I saw last night at the foot of the gangplank at the boat basin? He was mostly in shadow, but could it have been him? Are he and Lady Molly having a private ding dong? Was last night's game of hound and hare a waste of time? If it was, how would she dare try and profit from it when she meets Babe Lustig shortly. But Lady Molly was a very handsome piece. She could still win herself some whistles if she chose the right

134

street corners. 'Say Mack,' the familiarity camouflaging her inability to pronounce the name by which Lady Molly had earlier identified Uri, 'you in town on business or just a visit?'

Uri replied affably. 'A little of both.'

'It gets a little boring piloting this hack so I sometimes play a little game with myself. I try to guess my passenger's profession. You'd be surprised how often I hit the bull's eye.'

'I enjoy games,' said Uri with a quick flash of teeth, 'go ahead.'

'This is a really wild one. I got the feeling you have something to do with ships. You wouldn't be a sailor by any chance, would you?'

'Now isn't that remarkable. Isn't that quite remarkable, Molly?'

'Remarkable.'

'Then you're a sailor!' ejaculated Flo with triumph.

'Not by profession, no, but I do have master's papers.'

'Well you gotta admit that's close enough.'

'Flo.' Lady Molly said the name as though she was examining it for lice. 'You didn't by any chance follow me last night after we left Pauline's.'

Flo admirably kept her cool and said gruffly, 'Me?'

'I had the feeling you did. You were so concerned with my welfare at so late that hour, I wondered then if you might decide to keep a protective eye on me.'

'Well Lady Molly, I have to admit you're a little too smart for me. Yeah. I followed you till you caught that other cab. I wanted to make sure you was okay.'

'That was very thoughtful of you. Thank you.' Lady Molly and Uri exchanged a look. There wasn't a doubt in either mind that Lady Molly had been trailed to the boat basin. Lady Molly wondered if and when the information had been passed on to Sappho. Uri's face reflected an unusually placid lack of concern.

Flo had caught the quick silent exchange between Lady

Molly and Uri in her rear-view mirror. She felt unusually hot under her armpits and said nothing more until they arrived at *Checkpoint Charlotte*. Then she turned and said to them through the wire mesh, 'We've made port.'

Uri laughed while Lady Molly asked, 'Could you pick us up in about an hour, perhaps hour and a half.'

'No problem,' said Flo as she signalled thumbs up. 'I have one more job to do and then I'll be back here at Charlotte's hoisting a few at the bar. Just look for me when you're ready to leave.'

'I enjoyed your game very much,' said Uri loudly as he assisted Lady Molly from the vehicle.

'I got lots of them,' responded Flo, 'try me again some time.'

'Perhaps I will. Later.'

I could eat him raw, thought Flo as she pulled away.

Lady Molly took Uri's hand and started to lead him into *Checkpoint Charlotte's*. But Uri was an immovable object. 'What's wrong? It's not Flo, is it? I told you she was Sappho's paid informant. There's no reason not to proceed as planned.'

'I disagree. The poor little creature's death makes me feel it is imperative to move the schedule forward twenty-four hours.'

Lady Molly looked into Uri's strong face. 'Why?'

'It is known you were at the Potter girl's apartment to-day. Until this Michaela person is apprehended by the police, they will undoubtedly interrogate all other suspects. This will mean you and possibly myself.'

'I'd never say you were with me.'

'But we might have been seen together. Who can tell? How can we be sure? There must be no further delay. We have the keys.'

'We haven't the proof. You promised me you wouldn't make a move until you were absolutely sure.'

'A girl died for that letter.' He was moved by the pained expression on Lady Molly. 'You say this Belle Grady is an

136

intelligent person.'

'Intelligent enough to remove the letter from her office.'

'Let us hope she joins us tonight. Let us further hope we can learn from her what we need to know.'

'If there's anything to know.'

'I'm sure there is,' he said with lofty self-assurance, 'why else remove the letter?'

'Perhaps she was planning to do some homework,' said Lady Molly airily. 'And perhaps you're right about moving the operation forward. In the morning Miss Grady will have reason to suspect her office has been searched. She will then inform her friend Detective Mingus and so to hell with my conscience. Do as you feel you must.' She chuckled. 'After all, you *are* the captain of this ship and the crew shall obey his orders.' Then she added ruefully, 'And the devil take the hindmost. Shall we forget about dinner?'

'How can we when there's the hope Miss Grady will join us? We can spare these few hours. I will make the necessary phone call from this ...' he stared at the forebidding edifice, 'den of iniquity.'

'Uri my dear, it's nothing like that at all! Wait till you see. It's just like a kibbutz, if a bit more eccentric. Come along.' She led the way to the entrance. 'You have so much in common with the proprietress.'

'My God!' cried Uri Bar Ishiba once inside the premises, 'it is like a synagogue on the first night of Passover!'

'The analogy's not bad,' said Lady Molly indicating the press at the bar, 'they too ask the eldest at the feast "Why-for is this night different from any other". Ah! I see Charlotte! I think she recognizes me from last night!'

Behind the bar frenziedly mixing a pink lady, Reba the bartender was bellowing '*A wooo-man's a one-face....*' Miss Toklas the parrot hid her head under a wing while an irate woman with Buster Brown bangs and John Brown face (long mouldering in the grave) challenged her companion, 'Are you quoting from Mao Tse Tung or Mayo Methot?'

Charlotte pushed her way briskly through her cornucopia

of women with the corn cob pipe pointed straight ahead like a radar device. 'Ahoy there Duchess!' she greeted Lady Molly, 'welcome back aboard ship! Who's the bosun using your arm as a life raft?' Lady Molly made the introductions. Charlotte boomed, 'Pleased to meet you, Urine.'

'Uri,' said Uri politely.

'For short?' Charlotte thwacked him good-naturedly in the ribs.

'Urrf,' gasped Uri and Lady Molly suppressed a laugh.

'Belle and Tony Mingus are waiting at the table,' Charlotte shouted above the din of the crowd and Lady Molly flashed a happy smile at Uri who asked Charlotte if there was a telephone. 'You can use the one in my cage.' She turned and shouted, 'Hey Reba! My friend here wants to use the phone. Welcome him portside!'

Reba signalled acknowledgement and began a new serenade, '*None a-l-ooooone!*'

'Come on Duchess, I'll lead the way to the table while the boyfriend checks on his late date.' She cackled merrily while Lady Molly wondered if Charlotte knew she was psychic.

In a taxicab nearing *Checkpoint Charlotte*, Pat Drake bristled as she stared at the meter totalling what was beginning to look like the national debt. She growled to Malcolm, 'This is really outrageous. I'm going to get a licence and drive my own car.'

'You couldn't get a licence to use the I.R.T.'

'Innuendo and out the other and stop sulking! Think of what I've been *through* today.'

Malcolm's ears still ached from Pat's earlier marathon monologue detailing her involvement in Pauline Potter's death. He was not looking forward to an evening with Sappho and her hand maidens. He knew what to expect of the dinner conversation and was bored to tears with women's lib, gay lib and ad lib. He wished he was home snuggled up on his eight foot long sofa with a cold drink and a hot male prostitute. He was bored to tears with Pat Drake and her other lonely carbon copies and had lately taken to admitting he was bored to tears with himself.

'Of course,' trilled Pat, 'it will make an absolutely *mah*-vellous article. Now let me think, what magazine would pay the most for the *inside* story of Pauline's murder.'

'*Sports Illustrated*.'

'Do you think?' queried Pat innocently. 'Oh perk *up*,' she said with irritation to Malcolm, 'it's not as though we're joining the Last Supper!'

I've got news for you sweetie, Malcolm told himself, as far as I'm concerned it is.

Sappho's grey Rolls Royce deposited Babe Lustig on the dock at the foot of the street where Charlotte's place was located. It pulled away leaving Babe searching for a shadow in which to loiter until rendezvousing with Flo Hopper. Babe was loathe to admit to anyone but herself she was depressed and downhearted. She had never intended to kill Pauline. Her record had been clean for years, over twenty-five years. But she had never blundered before, and blundering was beneath contempt. She was getting old, that was it, old. There was insufficient preparation for burgling Pauline's flat. It should have been staked out. She should have phoned to see if Pauline was at home, or the room-mate. She should have listened at the bedroom door instead of making directly for the closet. Why had she ploughed ahead so desperately without foresight. *Desperately*. How often had she witnessed desperation undo others. She never dreamt she would one day fall into the trap herself. Brazil. *Gott In Himmel* Brazil. The elephant's graveyard of wandering fugitives. And all day long Willi will dance the samba with a bowl of fruit on her head and on her feet thick wooden wedgies. She groaned aloud. Of course there are rivers there filled with piranha. But of course! Her eyes blazed with fresh hope. One can always invite Willi for a swim and make sure she's the first one in.

Her ears were alerted again to the strange sound she had been hearing in the Rolls Royce en route to this destination. That eeerie *putt-putt-putt* like the sound of dredging engines. Then just as suddenly, there was quiet broken only by the lapping of water against wooden pilings. Where is Flo, she wondered. Why is she late? She strained her eyes at the radium dials of her wristwatch. Flo wasn't late. Babe was early.

'It's so noisy in here, I'm afraid you'll have to forgive me,' apologized Belle to Uri, 'but I didn't hear your last name.'

He enunciated carefully, 'Bar Ishiba.'

'Isn't it charming,' asked Lady Molly settled between Belle and Tony, 'it's a name that conjures up visions of Massada and Ararat and the wailing wall. And while we're on the subject of tears,' she said to Tony, 'have your men located Michaela Lorimer?'

Tony shook his head 'no', loath to speak in competition with the heated discussion underway at the next table involving five women blistering the atmosphere with a laudatory discussion of Sappho and the protest march. Lady Molly recognized the reason for his discomfort and said sympathetically, 'So much for their idol chatter.' Tony responded with a grateful smile while his eyes remained fixed on Uri who was giving a waiter his and Lady Molly's drinks order.

Belle asked Uri, 'Did you happen to see the demonstration on the library steps today by any chance?'

'Oh yes,' he said with a suave smile, 'I was there by Lady Molly's invitation.'

'What did you think of the mass strip-tease?' continued Belle. 'I'm sure a lot of people were repelled by it.'

Uri shrugged. 'I found it rather sad in a way. After all, man does not live by breasts alone.'

'I must have stood out like a sore thumb!' exclaimed Lady Molly. 'I wonder how many spectators wondered if I was the rebel in the ranks. But I couldn't have joined in if I wanted to. I wasn't wearing a brassiere.'

'Hey pal.' Uri met Tony's look. 'Were you the gent with Lady Molly when she went calling on Pauline?'

Belle sagged inwardly. Good old Tony. Lead him into a china shop and he'll grasp the invitation by both horns.

'Yes I was.' Uri took Tony's pitch without batting an eyelash, but it was Lady Molly who caught the ball.

'Why Belle my dear, didn't I mention that when I phoned you at the office?'

Belle permitted the ball to go wide past the plate. 'If you did it must have slipped my mind. I must admit all the while you were talking, my mind was on the letter.'

'Well so much for my so-called fascination!' said Lady Molly with a feigned archness that could have used further rehearsal. 'And now that you've brought it up, how far have you gotten?'

Belle sneaked a quick look at Tony and his face signalled 'green'. I managed to decipher about four words and a name. I've got them right here.' She opened her purse and found the scrap of note paper. 'Here it is. Now let me see. Well, there's "danger" ...'

'That must have whetted your appetite,' irrupted Uri.

'It *did*. Which reminds me I'm starving to death. Tony be a doll and catch a waiter.'

'What do I use for bait?'

Reba's falsetto penetrated across the room with '*I met a million dollah bay-beeeee ... in a four and nine cent store!*'

'And after "danger", what then?' persisted Uri.

'What?' inquired Belle blithely as though caught shoplifting, 'Oh of course ... after "danger". Well now let me see. I think I need glasses.' She held the paper away from her eyes as though suffering with sudden myopia. 'Oh yes. Then there's "pursuit" ... and oh look ... there's Pat and Malcolm!'

'How delightful.' Lady Molly sounded as though she'd just been invited to a funeral of an old foe. Pat had spotted the table and was semaphoring eagerly with a pink lace handkerchief which Malcolm insisted she tatted with her teeth. Lady Molly turned in her chair and was gratified to see Pat deep in conversation with Charlotte. There was no immediate danger of her besieging their company. She turned as Belle said:

' "Judgement".'

'I beg your pardon?'

' "Judgement",' repeated Belle with an endearing smile, 'that's the third word in the letter I deciphered.'

'Ah!'

'Um,' said Uri.

'Go ahead, tiger, let's hear the rest.' Tony might have been urging Joe Namath to a touchdown.

'Then we have "revenge" and "Bathsheba!" ' Belle heard a sudden snap and looked down. Uri had snapped in two a swizzle stick he had been toying with.

Lady Molly rattled off blithely, ' "Danger", "Pursuit", "Judgement", "Revenge", "Bathsheba" ... what a disconnected jumble!'

'Oh it connects if you try hard enough,' corrected Belle amiably. 'Listen to this sentence I worked up.' She cleared her throat and referred to the note paper like a lecturer at the Women's League who hoped she was more entertaining then Emily Kimbrough. ' "*You are in danger of the pursuit and judgement of the revenge sought by Bathsheba*" '. She looked up with an expression on her face which to Lady Molly appeared to beg a Pulitzer Prize. Uri was leaning back to permit the waiter room to serve his and Lady Molly's drink.

'When you find the strength,' Tony said to the waiter, 'bring us some menus.' The waiter hurried away with a perplexed expression trying to remember whether or not William Bendix was dead.

Lady Molly leaned toward Belle conspiratorially. 'You composed that sentence.'

'That's right. It wasn't easy but that's what I came up

with after a little juggling. It means nothing of course. But I found the four words and the name in the opening sentence of the letter and decided to try and see how they might link up and what you heard was the chain I devised. Not bad if I must say so myself.'

'Not bad at all,' said Uri without condescension.

'Hey Uri,' interrupted Tony, 'you come from that part of the world. Where does "Bathsheba" hit you?'

'I once knew a Bathsheba in Haifa, but all she ever pursued was a fair price.'

And then a deafening roar arose in the front of the room. The four looked about with bewilderment. They might have been spectators in the Coliseum a thousand years ago witnessing the entrance of the gladiators. It was Belle who first espied a radiant Sappho entering followed by Willi moving like the bouncing ball that scurried over lyrics flashed on movie theatre screens to the accompaniment of a Hammond organ. In a moment, Sappho and Willi were obscured as chairs were pushed back and Charlotte's clientele arose in a body to pay homage to their queen. Cheers and shouts and applause and hands slamming rapidly on tables and feet stomping assailed their ears as Lady Molly shouted into Belle's ear, 'Who came in.'

Belle told her with astringent succinctness, 'Sacco and Vanzetti.'

IX

While waiting for the din to subside, Lady Molly took the opportunity to study Belle and think about her with a fresh perspective. There was definitely more to her then met the eye and the ear. Last night's Belle Grady was unprepossessing and introspective, a square peg for the round hole of her elected profession. Now Lady Molly was beginning to investigate and understand the reverse of the dichotomy. Belle Grady publicly coloured her grey matter with discretion. Last night did not call for pyrotechnical displays of intellect. Like Lady Molly and Pat Drake, Belle hadn't jockied for a position to blow her own horn. She was an artist reserving her talent for the canvas, eschewing the idle doodling on a tablecloth. Belle's was an admirable self-confidence. She knew when to let the opposition know she was a worthy opponent. But was she positive of the identity of her opposition? Did she know how close she was to the key to this mysterious letter? Uri was smiling to himself. Was it for this effluvial display that was threatening to shatter her eardrums, or was he harbouring a similar respect for Belle Grady's achievement. He sensed she was looking at him and when their eyes met his smile broadened. Those chalcedonic eyes were flashing her a message which she quickly translated. Our move is not premature. We are dead on. Thank you, Belle Grady.

Lady Molly was amused to see Belle actually doodling. Was the artist frittering away the talent or making a calculation. Tony's face was a study. The notepaper on which Belle was making tiny marks had deliberately been placed in his line of vision. He abruptly reached over, crumpled the paper and shoved it in his pocket. Belle's cheeks were blazing as she helped herself to a large swig of her whisky. The

waiter reappeared with the menus and Tony accepted them
without interest. He had an appetite but there was nothing
in Charlotte's menu to satisfy it. He was forcing himself to
obey the four letter command Belle had hastily pencilled at
the bottom of the paper: *Wait.*

The room was settling down. Uproar subsided into hub-
bub. Charlotte was leading the Queen Bee and her drones
to their table. The cortege moved slowly. Sappho was stop-
ping to shake hands and receive impetuous embraces. Lady
Molly was disappointed no postulant humbled herself at
Sappho's feet. One walrus-faced woman tore a carnation
from her lapel and thrust it into Sappho's hands. Lady
Molly tore her monocle from her handbag and thrust it
into her eye. Someone was actually kissing the hem of
Sappho's dress. Perhaps a seamstress checking the crafts-
manship of the competition, Lady Molly consoled herself.

'Incredible,' said Uri, 'absolutely incredible. Golda
Meier will never believe it.'

'They've spotted us,' said Belle making it sound as
though they'd been lying in ambush.

'She is an unusually handsome woman, this Sappho,' said
Uri. 'But where could she have found that amazing little
creature who dances about like she's on a bed of hot
coals?'

'At the bottom of a box of crackerjacks,' said Belle. Willi
was appropriately fizzing and spluttering and giving off
sparks like the tail of the comet. Her hands were flying like
a catherine wheel gone berserk.

Uri beamed at Belle. 'You are a true epicure. You can
recognize a bad dish without sampling it.'

'It's been sampled,' said Belle candidly. 'We used to live
together. It wasn't an economical necessity, just a sad lapse
in judgement.'

'It happens to all of us,' sympathized Uri.

'I was touted off her by some friends. I should have
listened but who ever does at the time. The day she moved

145

in everything she unpacked was clean except her reputation.'

'Here they come,' muttered Tony.

Sappho arrived at the table like the vanguard of a Parisienne couturiere confident her Spring collection would win unanimous acclaim. She began in high C with 'Lady Molly what a delicious surprise' and then hit a cadenza with 'And with *Bale* of all people!' Belle felt as though she'd been caught in a compromising position with Madam Pandit. Willi went ominously quiet while Lady Molly introduced Uri and Tony.

'Won't you honour our table by joining us for a drink?' Uri's invitation settled around Sappho's head like a wreath of laurel leaves. Her eyes sparkled and she threw her head back to release a throaty laugh while Willi pointedly looked away from Belle.

'Get chairs,' Pat Drake ordered Malcolm and he returned the brusque command with a look that threatened instant annihilation. Charlotte had been watching the scene from her position in the cage foreseeing the emergency and dispatching two waiters to supply the accommodations.

'Oh Willi for heaven's sake let bygones be bygones,' chided Sappho. 'Just look at Belle. She's all smiles and friendly and the least you could do is acknowledge her greeting.'

'Miaow,' said Willi and Belle managed not to flinch.

'We are not amused,' said Sappho imperiously to Willi and then busied herself with the fresh seating arrangements as the waiters arrived with the chairs.

A very clever actress, Belle was thinking, or you've never met Uri Bar Ishiba before in your life. You betrayed no trace of recognition when you got a closer look at him or when you heard his name. There's not a trace of nervousness or unease in either Uri or Lady Molly's demeanor. We might be seated in a refrigerator the way everyone's keeping their cool. Even old reliable Mingus. He's genially ordering drinks like Diamond Jim Brady at an assignation

146

with Lillian Russell. Here he sits with a quorom of suspects, when will he turn the situation to his advantage?

'Say where's your buddy Lustig?' Tony trumpeted across the table to Sappho satisfying the last of Belle's private conjectures.

'She'll be along soon. You! Waiter!' She snapped her fingers at the willowy waiter of the previous evening. 'Dom Perignon!'

The waiter sashayed to her side and said saucily, 'I'm Clark Kent. Dom doesn't come in till later.'

'I'll have none of your cheek! Tell Charlotte I want two bottles of Dom Perignon from her private stock and be quick about it!'

'Get going sonny,' clipped Tony and the waiter moved away with a toss of golden curls.

'Wasn't it sad about poor Pauline,' interjected Belle.

'Dreadful! Absolutely dreadful!' Sappho might have been watching a souffle collapse. 'We heard it on the radio this evening.'

'I'd have thought you'd had a first hand account from either Lustig or the cat fancier next to you.' Sappho's chin dropped and Willi's face turned the colour of curdled pizza. Pat Drake gasped as though a shoulder strap might have just broken and Malcolm decided the evening might not be the bore he was sure it would be after all. Tony folded his hands on the table and continued. 'I got an eye witness what says Lustig and Willi here were at the scene of the crime within a few minutes of each other.'

'I didn't kill her!' blurted Willi.

'Be quiet Willi,' cautioned Sappho softly as she turned to Tony. 'I assume your witness is a reliable one.'

'He'd be acceptable in any court of law.'

'Good heavens!' irrupted Lady Molly in Belle's direction, 'then my eyes *didn't* deceive me. I *did* see Willi there this afternoon!'

Sappho studied Lady Molly as though she was a smear on a slide and then addressed Tony. 'Yes, Babe and Willi

147

were there.' Willi's stomach rumbled. 'You all know about the articles Pauline purloined from me. Babe and Willi were simply attempting to retrieve them.' She paused for a reaction but no one contravened. 'It's my property and I have every right to demand its return.'

'Aw what difference does it make anymore! After tomorrow ... oh!' Sappho kicked Willi under the table and Willi's mouth hung open like a nestling waiting for the worm to drop.

'What's tomorrow?' asked Tony suspiciously.

'Wednesday,' countered Sappho. 'What difference does it make who visited Pauline today? I thought it was obvious Michaela Lorimer killed Pauline in one of her dreadful drunken rages!'

'What's obvious can sometimes be deceptive,' said Belle.

Sappho chewed on the statement briefly and then said to Tony, 'Well whatever, this is hardly the time and place for interrogations, is it Mr. Mingus? I can assure you Babe and Willi will be available for questioning tomorrow or whenever you wish to call them in.'

'Well what the hell,' said Tony with a crooked grin, 'if we get it over with now, it can save us a lot of time and trouble. And we don't serve champagne at the precinct.' The waiters had arrived with the coolers containing the bottles of Dom Perignon.

'Wasn't *I* terribly cooperative?' inquired Pat coyly.

'Oh shut up!' snapped Sappho.

'The last time she shut up they had to call a doctor,' said Malcolm.

'*You* hush up!' and Pat concentrated on a waiter fumbling with the decorking. 'You're all thumbs,' she hissed to him.

'What's your story Willi?' Willi stared at Tony and then at Sappho and let her eyes glide past Belle to Tony.

'Well ... now let me think ... well you see ... it was like this. . . .'

148

A few moments after Babe looked at her wristwatch, Flo Hopper arrived and cut the engine. She reached over and opened the door and Babe moved in next to her on the front seat. Babe quickly pulled the door shut and they sat huddled together in darkness like pigeons in a church loft during a thunderstorm.

'What have you to tell me,' commanded Babe.

'Did you bring the green stuff?' Flo made a familiar gesture with thumb and index finger.

'Of course.'

'I'll take a hundred down.'

'I do not buy blind.'

'You'll buy this. It's a real juicer. A little something about a mutual friend.'

'What mutual friend?'

Flo examined a finger nail and then rasped, 'Lady Molly.'

Babe reached into her jacket pocket and brought out a roll of bills secured by a rubberband. 'You know better of course then to try and cheat Sappho.'

'Now have I ever tried to put one over on you girls?' Flo sounded like a tinhorn gambler. 'Peel the tens. You won't be sorry.'

'Let's start with that quartette of jungle babies.'

Detective Goldberg nudged Detective Kelly and indicated the garish black whores lined up outside a cafeteria. There was one in a yellow wig, one in a purple wig, one with her head swathed in a multicoloured bandana, and the fourth looked as though her hair had been charged with three thousand volts of electricity. Whether by chance or by design, they stood under a sign that announced 'Hot Dishes To Take Away'. As the detectives approached them, Yellow Wig nudged Purple Wig and warned, 'Fuzz.'

'Good evening ladies,' said Goldberg with the deceptively friendly voice of a television quiz master, and then flashed his badge.

'Lay off,' said Purple Wig huskily, 'we're clean.' She knew the detectives didn't believe her and in her present condition she could start an epidemic.

'Now don't be hostile,' said Goldberg as though reasoning with his mother-in-law. 'We just want a little cooperation. We're not looking to fill the police blotter. You girls may be able to help us and we'd appreciate your cooperation.' Kelly thought Goldberg ought to run for mayor. Goldberg quickly sketched in the purpose of their mission and he could tell from Purple Wig's reaction she had the information he needed. He decided to call his shot.

Purple Wig responded with, 'I don't want to get into any trouble.'

'Nobody's getting into any trouble. The girl may have been a witness to a murder, okay?'

Purple Wig rolled her eyes and then went into a whispered conference with Yellow Wig. To the practised eye of any Eighth Avenue denizen, it looked like the usual preliminaries to an eventual transaction. Neither girl particularly liked Chloe Waters. Chloe was in her decline and in desperation was causing a price war. There was no board of arbitration for whores and pimps and they had private means of eliminating unfair competition. Purple Wig emerged from the huddle and said, 'Now you didn't hear it from me, right?'

Goldberg formed an O with thumb and index finger.

'Her name's Chloe Waters. She's in the hamburger joint on the corner working on a score.'

'In an orange wig?' asked Kelly.

'No wig tonight, baby. And what you told us explains that. All us cats look the same in the dark except for the wigs. She's wearing a beaded cloche. Green blouse. Green hot pants and she's swinging a beaded bag. Keep your distance. The bag's loaded.'

'You're beautiful,' said Goldberg.

'Flatterer.'

Willi was finishing her impromptu testimony. 'And then I looked in and Pauline was laying face down with her hands and legs outstretched and I just got so frightened I ran away.'

'You're sure she was laying face *down*?' asked Tony with a note of scepticism.

'I swear to God.'

'But when I saw her. . . .'

'Quiet Pat,' barked Belle.

Sappho swiftly picked up the thread of conversation. 'That's exactly what Babe told me. The door was ajar so she went in and that's exactly how Pauline was lying on the floor.'

'Well then,' said Malcolm, 'then maybe Michaela is innocent!'

'Oh pooh!' sniped Pat, 'Pauline might have been taking a nap.'

Sappho suggested, 'Perhaps Pauline had been struck by Michaela sometime prior to Babe's arrival. Isn't that possible?'

'Possible,' said Tony. 'She already got a black eye from the girlfriend this morning. But from a preliminary examination of the body by the coroner, she wasn't dead more then maybe an hour or two before Pat arrived for her date with Pauline.' He turned to Lady Molly and Uri. 'You positively got no response when you went calling?'

'None whatsoever,' said Lady Molly.

'My dear!' said Sappho with astonishment, 'don't tell me you and your charming Uri were there too!'

'Pauline was expecting me,' Lady Molly told her.

'Poor Pauline. She was always such a stick in the mud. I'm so glad she started socializing before her untimely demise. Malcolm would you be a dear and refresh our drinks? Whatever can be keeping Babe. This is really tiresome and I want my dinner. Oh well, the best laid plans and all that nonsense. Tonight was by way of a celebration and instead we're holding this morbid post-mortem.'

'Lady, you're a real winner.' The subtle irony in Tony's voice did not go undetected by Belle.

'Oh *thank* you!' Sappho held her glass raised while Malcolm delicately tipped a bottle.

'Don't you give a damn about that letter anymore?' asked Tony.

'Oh but I do,' said Sappho blandly, 'but actually, it's really all been a tempest in a teapot. It was just a private note from my husband and really not all that important. I was merely furious that Pauline dare remove copies from my private file, that's all. After all it was in its way a criminal act. Do you have the letter?'

'No,' said Tony, 'I don't have the letter.'

They hadn't noticed Charlotte approaching. She leaned over and whispered in Tony's ear, 'Your office is on the phone, skipper.'

'Thanks Charlotte,' said Tony with a friendly pat on her rump. It felt like solid rock and Tony wondered if Charlotte was slowly petrifying. 'Excuse me,' said Tony to the others as he got up. He caught Belle's knowing look and then followed Charlotte to the telephone, picking their way with difficulty through the jam-packed room like the advance guard of an army platoon warily suspicious of hidden land mines.

Uri stroked his beard and chuckled. For a moment he resembled a wise rabbi pondering a question proposed by a precocious student. 'This is a most amazing experience. In my country when a murder is committed, all the suspects are herded together in the police station and subjected to a gruelling interrogation. But here! They sit around a table and sip champagne!'

'What do they serve in your territory?' asked Malcolm impishly, 'tea with lemon?'

'Tony always favours the casual approach,' explained Belle. 'I'm sure Lady Molly's told you I used to be associated with Tony on the police force.' Uri nodded. 'He's learned the hard way that gentle persuasion can often be

152

more effective.'

'Gentle pursuasion!' Sappho reared back as though she'd just been asked her age. 'Why he dove right in with questions the moment we were seated.'

'But wasn't he gentle?' Belle was grateful when Uri laughed.

'Isn't anybody hungry?' pleaded Lady Molly. 'I'm absolutely famished. I've had no lunch and I must admit I'm having a terribly difficult time digesting the present situation. Malcolm could I please see one of those menus?'

Malcolm was perusing one of the menus cut in the pattern of a ship's bell and exclaimed, 'Goodness, Reba must be doing the cooking tonight. They've got matzo ball soup.' He turned to Willi. 'Would you like some matzo ball soup?'

Willi grimaced and said, 'I'd prefer something from another part of the matzo.'

Tony had Goldberg on the other end of the phone and was straining to hear Goldberg's end of the conversation over the blaring juke box and the concerted cackle resembling a hen house in which the fowl were going berserk. 'Talk louder Goldberg,' shouted Tony, 'I can't beat the competition!'

Goldberg raised his voice several decibels. 'I have the witness. Her name is Chloe Waters. She's given us a statement. It ain't gonna win any prizes. She says when she and our missing party entered the premises, the victim was already lying on the floor in the position as described by Miss Patricia Drake. Michaela Lorimer was drunk having consumed a number of beers prior to transporting her companion to said premises on a motorcycle. Chloe Waters sized up the situation thusly and I quote, "I took one look at the stiff and got my hot tail out of there. I heard the score yelling something about oh my God what have I done and then headed down the stairs and knocked some broad on her ass on my way out". The broad what got knocked on her ass I am assuming is Miss Patricia Drake.' Goldberg

153

reached for a can of Pepsi Cola and refreshed his parched throat.

Tony wore a rueful expression as he said into the phone, 'Okay, release Chloe Waters but be sure you know where to find her when we need her. Hey Goldberg, don't go away. You there?'

'I'm here! I'm here!'

'Is Marchetta there? Did he reach Liz Bancroft?'

'That is the next subject on the agenda. Bancroft was contacted half an hour ago and wanted to know your present position which was duly relayed to her. She is joining you at *Checkpoint Charlotte* and please order her a double scotch with one cube of ice.'

'You got the coroner's report yet?'

'That is the third item on the agenda. Shall I read it to you?'

Tony's voice went brittle. 'Unless you can fly it down by carrier pigeon.'

Goldberg cleared his throat and began reading off the coroner's report.

The arm around Flo Hopper's neck looked thick and juicy like underdone roast beef and Flo sank her teeth into it. Babe grunted as Flo fought to struggle loose while managing to force open the door on her side.

'You will not cheat us!' shouted Babe. 'Your information is worth nothing! Give me back the money!'

'Up you!' gasped Flo as two fingers connected with one of Babe's eyes. Babe yelped with agony relaxing her grip on Flo to attend to the injured orb and Flo took her opportunity and scrambled out of the taxicab. Thank God for Enna Jettick shoes thought Flo as she tore off in search of sanctuary.

With tears streaming from the injured eye, looking like an enraged Cyclops, Babe forced open the door on her side and heaved her huge bulk out of the vehicle. She swiped at the bad eye with the sleeve of her jacket and then steadied herself with both hands on the fender to gain her bearings.

154

She could dimly discern Flo disappearing in the direction of Charlotte's place. Babe snorted like a tramp elephant at the scent of the spoor and pushed herself erect.

'Ooooff!' grunted Babe as she suddenly staggered forward.

What hit me, she wondered as she struck the ground with the impact of a mack truck colliding into a cement wall. She shook her head and then looked over her shoulder and saw Michaela Lorimer looming over her with fists clenched, feet spread apart, an avenging Goliath. Even in the dim light from the tiny bulb in the interior of the taxi Babe could recognize the look of murder.

'I'm gonna kill you!' Michaela took a flying leap for Babe with fingers tensed and outstretched. Babe swiftly rolled to one side and Michaela crashed to the pavement. Babe grabbed Michaela's head in a hammerlock while Michaela's elbow connected with Babe's groin. Babe treated her adversary to a welcome cry of pain and momentarily relaxed her grip. Michaela twisted around and her legs deftly caught Babe around the waist in a painfully tight scissor's grip. Perspiration began dripping from the pores on Babe's forehead as her fingers desperately groped for a vulnerability. She found Michaela's ankle and brutally treated it like a bottle cap. Michaela yelled and brought a fist down on Babe's head. Babe moved quickly and caught the hand and with an amazingly agile movement threw Michaela into a somersault. Michaela flew through the air with the greatest of ease and landed face down on the roof of the taxi. Babe struggled to her feet while cursing her smarting eye and emitted a bellow that sent a nearby flock of starlings heading south a month before the season. Michaela crouched on hands and knees with leg muscles taut for a leap. Babe moved back slowly to steel herself for the awaited impact. It came in a flash and Babe staggered back against a piling, hit her head but managed to catch Michaela in a ferocious bear hug. For several seconds they rolled on the ground like a pair of passionate mastodons.

155

Michaela struggled desperately. She could feel her rib cage beginning to give and she took the only opportunity that afforded itself. She sunk her strong teeth into Babe's neck drawing sufficient blood to keep a vampire in vitamins for a week. Babe screamed and hurled Michaela back with a tremendous impetus that sent Michaela across the hood of the taxi and head first through the windshield.

Blood streaming from her neck, Babe staggered to the taxi, pulled back the door, reached in for Michaela's bleeding, lacerated head, grasped it firmly with both hands, and with all the weight she could muster, pressed down. Michaela emitted a short rattle and then went limp. Babe staggered back and then sank to the ground in a sitting position.

Somewhere a seagull screeched and a fog horn moaned morosely. Babe raised her hands in front of her face and wondered, who'd have thought Michaela had so much blood in her. And then to her astonishment, she realized she was blacking out. There was no controlling it. She was defence-less from fright and exhaustion. Her hands dropped, her head dropped, and then she dropped. Her body settled into a grotesque sprawl looking like a piece of avant-garde sculpture donated to the Museum of Modern Art by a quixotic benefactor.

Behind the bar in *Checkpoint Charlotte*, Reba the bar-tender was in top form. With one hand pressed to her stomach and the other flat behind her back, she was doing a nimble hornpipe while mellifluously caroling '... *Thirteen men on a dead man's chest....*'

'*Cut off their balls! Cut off their balls!*' counterpointed Miss Toklas the parrot flapping her wings and sending a welcome current of air in the direction of Flo Hopper who was downing her second straight gin. Her position was camouflaged by fifty women and a select assortment of males and when not contemplating a solution to her predicament caught the odd snatch of conversation. On her left a skeletal

156

young man with matted hair cascading to just below his shoulders was telling an owlish-faced woman, 'My dear Flora, things are so awful in Hollywood even the tennis courts are empty!'

On her right a woman whose loose-limbed posture gave the impression she'd been constructed from an erector set was warning an obese and hirsute companion, 'Watch out for that guy waving a finger at you. He's a proctologist.'

'I can't spend the weekend with you,' Flo heard behind her, 'I don't have the right clothes.'

'Baby, you won't need any clothes.'

Flo signalled the one-woman floorshow for another gin and found the courage to stand on tip toe in search of a friendly and helpful face. Babe probably hadn't followed her into Charlotte's because she knew it was no place to create a scene. That meant she was waiting for Flo to emerge and Flo wasn't emerging without a bodyguard. While scanning the room she heard a voice as lush as a prolonged arpeggio from a Hawaiian guitar insisting, 'He may be Freud in theory but I know he's Jung at heart.'

When Tony returned to the table he said to Belle loudly and deliberately so that the others could hear, 'Michaela Lorimer's clean.' Sappho concentrated her attention on the waiter depositing plates of fried chicken and french fried potatoes on the table. Her insouciance was deceptive only to Willi who was digging into Malcolm's potatoes like a Colorado beetle determined to destroy the crop.

Belle glibly returned Tony's serve. 'That puts a new complexion on the case.'

'How do you mean "clean"?' interrupted Uri with his head cocked inquisitively.

'She didn't kill Pauline. I just got the coroner's report. Pauline's heart collapsed.'

Sappho moved in quickly. 'I should have thought of that. Pauline had a very bad heart condition. She was such a bundle of nerves I once tried to put her on tranquillizers but she said they made her gag.'

Tony was talking before Sappho finished her sentence. 'Somebody or something put a fright in her that was too much for her to take.' Then he acknowledged Sappho. 'But I'll tell you this. There was a fractured bone in her neck and I'm giving odds your henchwoman Babe did *that*.'

'But I told you Babe said....'

'*You* told me what Babe said. I want to hear it from *Babe*. I thought you said she was joining you here. Where is she? Or were you stalling for time while your Brunhilde takes it on the lam?'

Sappho slammed her champagne glass on the table and Belle was amazed the stem didn't crack. 'Be careful when you make wildcat accusations, Mr. Mingus. The man doesn't live who can intimidate me. *Willi!* Go outside and find Babe!'

'Where?' asked Willi innocently while munching on a spud.

'Will you please stop acting the fool! You're beginning to nauseate me.'

'That's not acting,' said Malcolm drily to no one in particular.

'Don't you say things like that to me!' snarled Willi baring teeth and shredded potatoes.

'Why here's Flo!' said Lady Molly in a piercing voice that might also have brought birds and dogs.

Sappho's head swivelled as Flo moved past her to Tony and Belle. 'Flo!' she commanded, 'where's Babe? Where did you leave Babe?'

'She's out there someplace!' barked Flo. Like Cerberus guarding the gates, thought Lady Molly. 'Tony you gotta help me. The fat bitch just tried to strangle me!'

Sappho was half out of her seat with uncontrollable anger and leaning across the table, her chest heaving melo-dramatically but rhythmically. 'You're lying!'

'Lying my behind.' Flo put an unsteady hand on Tony's shoulder. 'Be a pal and get me back to the cab. She's on the warpath and it's my scalp she's after.'

'Poor old Flo,' said Belle after clucking her tongue, 'you have met your moment of truth at last. What piece of info did you overcharge for now?'

Lady Molly brightened and crowed as though the sun was about to rise. 'Why she's been telling Babe about my visit to the yacht last night!'

Sappho sank back into her chair. 'What yacht?'

'The yacht I'm travelling on,' contributed Uri. 'It's moored at the Seventy-Ninth Street boat basin.'

'Hey!' hey'd Willi eagerly, 'that's where the Burtons were docked!'

'Wasn't that it?' Lady Molly asked Flo.

'Oh hell!' cried Flo, 'I'm going straight after tonight. Yeah yeah yeah! Here!' She flung the wad of greenbacks on the table near Sappho. 'Take it. I don't want it. Tony ... *please*!'

'Pull up a chair Flo and have a drink,' said Tony affably, 'there ain't no rush. I got some unfinished business here.'

Flo looked about bewilderedly but there wasn't a vacant chair in sight. 'I'll go back to the bar and wait,' she said weakly.

'*Malcolm!*' Malcolm snapped his head to Pat Drake. 'Get Flo a chair!'

' "Malcolm get a chair"! "Malcolm get a chair"! That's all I ever hear! "Get a chair"! "Get a chair"! What the hell am I supposed to be? An usher at a Presbyterian church service? Hey you! Waiter! Yes *you*, you dessicated Goldie Hawn!' His voice lowered to the surprising basso profundo. 'Go get us a chair and don't stop to cruise the toilet!' He turned to the others with his arms folded and said with a magnificent air of supremacy, 'You should know that inside every queen there's a truckdriver struggling to get out. *Stop eating my potatoes!*' His palm made a three-point landing on the back of Willi's hand.

'Ouch!' yelled Willi. 'Just for that I'm going home!'

'Go find Babe!' shouted Sappho.

'Sappho, Sappho,' Lady Molly cautioned, 'everyone's

looking at us. Do lower your voice. Uri, Sappho's glass needs refilling.'

'Hey Malcolm,' said Tony jovially, 'I hate to tell you this but we need one more chair.'

'Who for? The Holy *Ghost*?'

'No, Liz Bancroft.' Tony turned to the others. 'I forgot to tell you she was joining us.'

'How pleasant,' said Uri pleasantly, 'that makes ten of us. Now we have a *minion*.'

All but Lady Molly and Uri turned to ferret out Liz Bancroft. She was standing somewhat unsteadily at the edge of the dining area casing the room for Tony and Belle. While she was slightly high, her clothes were completely sober. She wore a navy blue Nina Ricci suit with a small cameo pinned above her right breast. She carried a navy blue handbag which she waved over her head in recognition when she espied Belle.

'Oh lookie there,' a voice simpered as Liz weaved her way between the tables, 'we have a real live celebrity.'

Liz turned to spear her victim. 'I thought Radclyffe Hall was dead.' She grabbed the back of the nearest chair and held on to it until she found Belle again and then proceeded warily on her way as though the floor was inlaid with fresh eggs. She recognized Pat and Malcolm and then with a short intake of breath, Sappho and Willi. Lady Molly and Uri sat with their backs to her.

Belle whispered to Tony, 'Go get her. I think she's pissed.'

As Tony got up, Belle's eyes wandered and framed Lady Molly and Uri. Lady Molly was saying something to Uri under her breath and Belle could see the muscles in his jaw working. She next saw Tony reach Liz and greet her as he took her arm. Liz's sombre expression remained frozen as she permitted herself to be guided to the others. When they reached the table, Tony asked Liz, 'Do you know everybody here?'

'She certainly knows me!' cried Lady Molly extending

160

her hand to Liz. 'She interviewed me on my arrival the day before yesterday. This is my friend Uri Bar Ishiba.' Uri shot out of his seat like a projectile and made a grab for Liz's hand.

'I am so pleased to meet you. Only this evening I had the pleasure of watching you on television. I admire the manner in which you treated the protest march.'

'And how was *that*?' thundered Sappho who had forgotten about watching the news due to the incident with Willi.

'Delicately,' over-enunciated Liz. Uri still clung to her hand and her eyes moved and met his. 'So nice to meet you Mister Bah Isheeboo.' He released her hand and she stared at it as though it had been freshly gilded with gold plate. Then she noticed Belle's smile and made a graceful gesture with her hand. 'You beam like a beacon in the night, Miss Grady. May I sit next to you and cadge a sip of your scotch? I gather mine wasn't ordered.'

Belle made room as the harassed waiter struggled to wedge another chair into place. 'If you're expecting anybody else,' he said with a haughty, mincing air, 'you'll have to use K.Y.'

Sappho was in control of herself again and oozed charm as she spoke to Liz. 'And to what do we owe the unexpected pleasure of your company?'

Liz had confiscated Belle's glass. 'I was seen at Pauline's this afternoon.'

'Another one!' exclaimed Malcolm. 'Somebody should have been selling tickets!'

X

Liz threw her head back to release a gust of laughter.

'What were you doing there?' Tony asked her when the laughter subsided.

'I heard about a letter and decided to try and lay my hands on it. After all, Sappho's big news and that's what I'm paid for.'

'You give it back to her!' yelped Willi with her tiny fists clenched and beating the table ineffectually.

Liz's eyes went lethal. 'I *loathe* you.'

'Oh!' gasped Willi and Malcolm caught her chair as it started to tip over.

Liz turned to Belle with an overexaggerated smile. 'I said it and I'm glad.'

'I'll get you some black coffee,' Tony said to Liz.

'I have already bathed, thank you,' she riposted. 'I was having a quiet booze-up at home when your Detective Maraschino ...'

'Marchetta....'

'... That's your story ... contacted me and I thought it was mighty nice of me to come down to this perfectly odious psychedelic harem and tell you what little I know and my God will you look at the creatures in this room. Do they all subsist on ugly pills?'

'Liz what can I get you?' Belle asked.

'A carriage drawn by six of these misanthropic odour-lisques.' Drink had not dulled her sesquipedalian powers and she was enjoying herself enormously. 'Well sport,' she suddenly said to Tony, 'whom am I expected to rat on?'

'Depends on what you saw.'

'I am about to break your heart you magnificently unique creature. I didn't see a god damn thing.'

'Did you talk to Pauline?' persisted Tony.

'No I did not talk to Pauline.'

'Well what *did* you do?'

'Would you believe I peeked through the keyhole?'

'I believe, I believe, what did you see?'

'Another eye?' suggested Malcolm. Tony glared at him and Malcolm explained, 'Well we could use a laugh.'

'I saw nothing,' said Liz, 'because undoubtedly the key was in the keyhole.'

'Did you hear anything?'

Liz was focusing on a ship's model projected on a wire over her head. 'I suppose I heard something.'

'Come on Liz,' urged Tony impatiently.

Liz suddenly slammed her hand down on the table. 'The only voice I recognized was Pauline's. I don't know who the other two ...' she paused and then added swiftly, '... were.'

'Two,' said Tony.

'Two,' repeated Belle.

Tony put his hand under Liz's chin and directed her face towards his. Tears were welling up in her eyes and her nostrils were quivering. 'How long did you listen at the door,' he asked gently.

'I ... I ...' She slapped his hand away and hid her face in her hands and sobbed softly.

Sappho broke the embarrassed silence. 'Willi, please fetch Babe and tell the chauffeur to pull up at the door.' She turned to Tony, 'Unless you have any objection I would like to leave.'

'I got no objection after I talk to Babe Lustig. And in case you're getting any funny ideas, some of my boys are parked in a car across the street by now. Nothing serious on my mind. Just a precautionary measure. I still think Lustig did the job on Pauline's neck. Just a hunch mind you, but if she did, it'd go easier on her if she admitted it. One of your high-powered lawyers can take over after that. I'm sure he'll get her off easy.'

'I'll go look for her,' volunteered Belle.

'Oh no you won't!' said Willi rising. 'Sappho asked *me*!'

Belle rose to the occasion merrily. 'Why don't we go together sweets, and discuss your favourite brand of frozen food.'

Willi's face reddened as she said with an ineffective bravura, 'I'm not afraid of you.'

'There's no reason for you to be,' said Belle circling the table to Willi's side, 'I only slap mosquitoes when they bite. Let's go!'

'Ain't Belle a great broad?' Tony asked the others with pride. Liz had blown her nose in Belle's napkin and as she dabbed at her nose said to Tony, 'She's too good for the average man.'

Tony patted her gently on the back. 'Want to tell me the rest.'

'There's nothing more to tell. I wasn't there more then a minute when I decided to make tracks and I left. That's my story and I'm sticking to it.'

And I'm sticking to it. Tony had heard those words too often not to realize Liz Bancroft was guilty of the sin of omission but he didn't press the point.

Uri was looking at his wristwatch and Lady Molly had a questioning look on her face which Uri caught. He nodded and smiled as though to assure her time was still on their side. Sappho saw the pantomime between them from the corner of an eye and then asked Malcolm to order another bottle of champagne. Liz turned to Pat Drake and asked, 'Heard any good jokes lately?' Pat took the question seriously and said she hated jokes. Liz told her she hated people who told jokes and Malcolm screamed at a waiter to bring him a cold compress for his throbbing temples. A wizened old lady approached Sappho for her autograph and when she spoke turned out to be a wizened old man. Tony thought he looked awful wearing the tiara.

Outside Charlotte's, Belle waved a friendly greeting to the four detectives in the unmarked car parked on the opposite side of the street. The air was chill and damp and a grim mist had settled in from the river. Belle hurried to catch up with Willi and when she did, put her arm through Willi's in a friendly gesture. Willi rudely jerked her arm free.

'Cool it, Willi,' said Belle, 'I'm sorry about what happened yesterday. We can still be friends, right?'

Willi's heels click-click-clicked on the pavement and without seeing her face, Belle instinctively knew it was coloured with petulance. 'I suppose we can,' said Willi in a little girl voice, 'it doesn't cost anything.' She suddenly stopped and confronted Belle. 'Listen, Tony can't really prove Babe cracked Pauline's neck, can he?'

'You know Tony never talks until he has the proof behind him. He also knows you saw more then you told.'

'I told the truth!'

'The hell you did.'

'I thought we were friends again.'

'We are if you behave like one.'

'Then don't be mean to me.' They resumed walking at a slow, measured pace. 'All right I'll tell you, but I don't want you to screw up any of our plans.'

'What plans?'

'That's for me to know and you to find out.'

Belle had been warned when she met Willi that when opposites attract it can sometimes lead to a delayed collision, but the Willi she had met two years ago had seemed deceptively innocent, loving and naive, and it was the gentleness and softness that attracted Belle to her. It was only gradually after a period of a year she came to recognize that the cosy exterior camouflaged a will of iron. She endured the remainder of the relationship with the faint hope of a metamorphic miracle, but if one was developing, it had been arrested by the advent of Sappho. Willi had definitely not improved. If anything, there was an unpleasantly perverse regression.

'All right, tell me the truth Willi.'

165

'You promise I won't get into trouble?'

If only you knew you are already drowning in a sea of slime. 'I give you my word.'

'Okay. I trust you. Well, I opened Pauline's door a little because it wasn't locked and I saw Babe with one hand over Pauline's mouth and the other hand gripping her neck by the back and shaking the hell out of her. Then I heard a noise from the other apartment and I didn't know what to do, so I ran upstairs to the next floor and waited until I heard Babe leave. In fact, I kinda took a quick peek to make sure it was Babe leaving and it was. Then I went back down and I looked in the room and there was Pauline stretched out on the floor face down with her arms and legs sprawled out. So you see, that part was true. And then I went home to tell Sappho and ...' The memory of her earlier indignation at the hands of Sappho and Babe suddenly overwhelmed her and she came to an abrupt halt under a street lamp situated on the corner.

'What's the matter?'

'Nothing,' she said in a quivering voice.

Belle grabbed her wrist. 'What happened when you told Sappho?'

'I can't tell you. Sappho would never *forgive* me'

'What happened?' Belle's grip tightened. 'Shall I get Tony to ask you?'

'*No!*'

'Then come on, spill.' Willi told her. Belle whistled and then said, 'Those are certainly one pair of frightened ladies.'

'Sappho isn't afraid of *anything*!' Willi claimed staunchly.

'You know, Willi, of late I just might think you're right. At this very moment I even begrudge her a bit of admiration.'

'What do you mean?' Belle said nothing and Willi was annoyed, and annoyance made Willi brag. 'Oh I don't care what you mean. Tomorrow we're going to Brazil!'

'Oh? Brazil?'

166

'Brazil South America.'

'Babe may not be permitted to leave the country, you know.'

'Oh.' Willi was deflated. 'Sappho will think of something.'

'I'm sure she's thinking right now.'

'Come on. I see Flo's cab. See? The doors are open and hey....! *Hey!* Somebody's laying across the hood and the windshield looks smashed!' Willi was running to the parked vehicle with Belle pacing her alongside. Willi was the first to reach the taxi and screamed. 'Oh! Oh! Oh! Oh!' she repeated like a patient without novocaine under a dentist's drill. Belle widened the door of the cab, kneeled for a better look at the face of the nearly decapitated head and recognized Michaela Lorimer.

'Oh Christ,' she murmured. She backed away gasping for air watching Willi who stood with her face hidden in her hands. 'Oh my Christ,' repeated Belle. Where's Babe, she then wondered. Where has she fled to. Belle renewed herself and circled the body sprawled across the hood and saw Babe lying on the ground, her face and hands and clothes an ugly mass of coagulating blood. 'Willi!'

'*What?*'

Belle rushed to her and pulled her hands away from her face. 'Go get the boys in the car. Hurry!' Willi raced away. Belle fumbled in her jacket pocket and found cigarettes and matches and with trembling hands managed to get a cigarette into her mouth. After five quick swipes at the flint, the match ignited and Belle applied the flame and took a deep drag. It was then she wondered if Babe Lustig was dead. She returned to the prone figure and knelt at Babe's side. Belle struck another match and the full sight of Babe's bloodstained head and face filled her with a revulsion she hadn't felt since the mass mammarian display earlier in the day. She forced herself to lift one of Babe's eyelids. The eyeball was bloodshot and Belle was sufficiently trained to recognize the symptoms of a fractured skull. She released

167

the eyelid and got to her feet as she heard the prowl car pull up. Detective Kelly was the first to reach her. He barked an order over his shoulder for an ambulance and Belle hastened back to Charlotte's. Willi hadn't returned with the detectives and now there was undoubtedly chaos back at their table in *Checkpoint Charlotte's.*

'Holy Mother of God,' Belle heard Kelly say as she hurried away, 'I wish I'd seen the fight!'

Holy Mother of God I'm glad I didn't, thought Belle. Poor stupid Michaela. Poor pathetic Pauline. Apartment available on lower Ninth Avenue now going cheap. Previous tenants suddenly relocated.

Ahead of her, Belle saw Tony rushing to meet her. Behind him, a solid corps of humanity was erupting from Charlotte's like a street gang alerted to an emergency rumble.

Tony reached Belle and grabbed her by the shoulders. 'Is Lustig dead?' he barked.

'I don't think so,' said Belle in a low, breathless voice. 'I think she's got a bad concussion. Go see for yourself.'

Tony sped away from her and Belle stood momentarily frozen as the crowd from Charlotte's scenting blood surged past her like early-bird bargain hunters besieging a department store. Then she saw Sappho arriving followed by Willi, Pat Drake, Flo and Malcolm.

'My hack! What the Christ have those bull dikes done to my hack!' yelled Flo as she went sprinting past reminding Belle of a giraffe in flight.

Belle grabbed Sappho's arm. 'Don't go. It's very ugly.'

'Babe ... what about Babe? She's not *dead*?' Sappho's face was alabaster white. Like Rider Haggard's legendary heroine, Sappho seemed to have aged twenty years in five minutes.

'No. There's an ambulance on the way. She's in pretty bad shape.'

'Pretty bad shape,' echoed Sappho staring past Belle, sounding like the ghostly emission of a thing that goes

168

bump in the night. Sappho jerked her arm free. 'I have to go to her. I can't leave her like this.'

'Somebody go with her,' Belle said in the general direction of the semi-circle that consisted of Willi, Pat and Malcolm. Willi whimpered and backed away. Malcolm squared his fragile shoulders, took Sappho by the arm and led her to the scene of carnage.

'Where are the others?' Belle asked Pat.

'I guess they're still sitting there, dear. Liz got hysterical when Willi came flying in like Chicken Little to announce the sky was falling.'

Belle took her hand. 'Come back in with me.'

'Happily!' exploded Pat. 'Is it as ghastly as Willi described it?' She trotted behind Belle like a miniature poodle.

'If I was going on a diet, I'd be grateful for what I just saw.'

Pat shuddered and followed Belle back into Charlotte's place. Pat's eyes found the table and was satisfied Lady Molly and Uri were still there with Liz. Liz was hunched over the table, her body shaking with sobs and Lady Molly was attempting to ply her with a glass of whisky. Charlotte stepped into Belle's path.

'Shiver me timbers, girl, is it as bad as it's been piped?'

'Worse.' She tried to move past her but Charlotte had a strong grip on her arms.

'Them's bad tidings, girl. The fuzz have been trying to close me down for months. They can't link that blood bath to me, can they? They won't shoot dirty pool and try to frame me on this will they?' Charlotte's voice blended in Pat's ears with the wail of the ambulance siren outside. Pat looked at Belle whose eyes were glued at the table beyond Charlotte. Uri had moved to Liz and seemed to be trying to reason with her about something. Liz was shaking her head back and forth violently and Lady Molly had directed the glass of whisky to her own mouth. Charlotte screeched like Miss Toklas, 'Belle for chrissakes you gotta help me! All my pieces of eight are tied up in this hulk!'

'I'll help ... I'll help!' Belle shouted in irritation. 'I'll get Tony to straighten it out for you!' Belle jerked free and hurried to the table.

The scene at the dock had been too much for Malcolm's tender stomach. He stood at one side retching while a sympathetic waiter held his head tipped forward. Malcolm had heard Tony say to Detective Kelly after surveying Michaela and Babe, 'Well this is certainly self-explanatory.' He might have been a butcher in an abattoir discussing the choice cuts.

Sappho was kneeling at Babe's side repeating her name over and over again in a variety of hysterical inflections but like the Sphinx, Babe was in no condition to respond. The ambulance pulled up at the scene followed by two patrol cars, the ambulance disgorging two attendants with a stretcher. Tony was ordering the small crowd to disperse while back at Charlotte's Reba the bartender was mentally tabulating the probable deficit of payment of outstanding bar tabs.

Tony went to Sappho and helped her to her feet. 'You're wasting your time. She'll be out for a long time.'

Sappho looked into his face and he was surprised to see her capable of compassion. 'Where will you take her?'

'Bellevue.'

'Bellevue.' Sappho stared away to the river and after a few seconds said, 'I will go with her.'

Tony was slowly walking her away. 'I think it's better you go home.'

'Home?' Sappho sounded as though she had forgotten her address.

'Yeah, home. There's nothing you can do at the hospital. I'll call you later and let you know how Babe's doing.'

Malcolm had recovered and fell into step with Tony and Sappho. 'Babe,' Sappho said in a far away voice. 'My poor Babe. Lying there in that filth. That she should come to this. I have seen it for myself but I cannot fathom it! Not

170

Babe. This cannot have happened to Babe.'

'Malcolm,' Tony said over Sappho's head, 'see that she gets home.' They had reached the street lamp and Malcolm's face was ash grey and sunken and Tony wondered if he should assign Sappho a sturdier escort.

'Sappho! *Sappho!*' Willi emerged from a shadow with a tear-stained face.

'Make yourself useful,' said Tony to Willi sharply. 'Get her out of here. Take her home.' He relinquished his position at Sappho's side to Willi who put an arm around Sappho's waist and stared beseechingly at her idol's immobile face. He started to move away when Sappho spoke his name as though she had tossed a hot rivet.

'Babe is dying, isn't she?' She spoke with the icy calm of a broker writing off a bad investment.

Tony wasn't sure if Babe was dying or not but he grasped the opportunity. 'Yeah, I think she's had it. Now I'd appreciate the truth about her at Pauline's today.'

'Yes, yes you're right Tony.' A Shakespearian tragedienne would have bristled with envy at the dramatic delivery. 'I can only repeat what Willi told me. Babe did throttle Pauline. Isn't that what you told me, Willi?'

'Yeah!' responded Willi eagerly. 'I told it all to Belle just now!' She missed Sappho's look of a boa constrictor about to swallow a native bearer. 'Belle can tell you everything.'

They heard the banshee wail of the ambulance siren as it tore past them with its morbid cargo. Sappho turned and saw the vehicle flash past in the vanguard of two patrol cars. The thrill-seekers and the curious were shuffling past them returning to Charlotte's like satisfied cormorants. Some paused to offer their sympathies and speak a few encouraging words to Sappho, but she made no acknowledgements. Her eyes were fixed on the departing cortege and her graceful fingers were stroking her temple in a gentle massage. Detective Kelly found Tony and they moved away for a private discussion.

'My cab's a wreck!' Flo Hopper shouted as she came purposefully striding towards Sappho and her two attendants. 'You're gonna pay for this Sappho! You should see the upholstery for God's sake!'

'Oh go away!' squeaked Willi in a Minnie Mouse voice, 'you've got insurance, haven't you?' Sappho ignored Flo and started walking briskly to the Rolls Royce parked a hundred yards ahead.

'Up you Sappho!' sneered Flo. 'You ain't nothing without your biggest sister of them all!'

Willi's head swivelled and she spat, 'Communist!'

The waiter sidled up to Malcolm and inquired dulcetly, 'Would you like to come to my place later and pull yourself together?'

Malcolm's eyes widened with the shock of the unexpected invitation, looked the waiter up and down and retorted with a vixen expression, 'My dear, I am not seeking the kindness of strangers!'

Tony returned from his conference with Kelly and signalled Malcolm to follow him back to Charlotte's. As Sappho and Willi were about to pass the entrance, Lady Molly and Uri came hurrying out. Lady Molly hurried into Sappho's path. 'Sappho, my poor dear Sappho. Belle told us. It's absolutely horrible. Is there anything I can do?'

Sappho drew herself up regally. 'When the curtain descends, Lady Molly, there is nothing left but for the actors and the audience to depart.'

If this was meant as a rebuff, Lady Molly chose to ignore it though she was tempted to remind Sappho that before actors depart they usually remove their make-up. 'Would you like me to come with you? You really shouldn't be alone at a time like this.'

'She has *me*,' irrupted Willi. Lady Molly flashed her a look that spoke sympathy for Sappho's poverty.

Sappho signalled her chauffeur and then turned to Lady Molly. 'Thank you Molly, there's no need to put yourself out.' The Rolls Royce crawled to a halt and Malcolm reached for the rear door and opened it. Sappho swept into the back seat followed by Willi. Uri moved to Lady Molly's side and together they watched the automobile pull away. Flo vulgarly spat at the ground and then entered Charlotte's. Tony had placed himself in front of Lady Molly and Uri.

'Why don't you two join me for a night cap. I think we can all use one. What do you say?' The invitation held the implication of a command.

'I'm afraid there's no time now,' said Uri curtly. His voice was a mixture of impatience and urgency as though he was hurrying to catch a train.

'You'll have to make the time,' said Tony flatly. 'It could save us all a lot of trouble if you two spill what went on with Pauline.' Uri started to remonstrate but Tony over-rode him. 'Look, I don't believe a word of your alibi. Liz Bancroft overheard two voices with Pauline and the only double act Pauline entertained was you and Lady Molly.' Again Uri attempted to remonstrate. 'Okay okay! I know! Bancroft's drunk. On that score she might not hold up as a reliable witness. But we're not in court now. I'm asking you as friends to level with me so I can lock this thing up.'

'The gentle persuasion,' said Lady Molly with a smile of admiration. 'Belle knows everything Tony. We've told her everything. I am at your disposal in the morning and I promise you I will go through all the necessary official motions. But please don't detain us any longer. Please don't.'

'*Tony!*' Belle came hurrying into the street. 'Let them go. I've got everything you want. Pat Drake heard it and what more do you need. Just let them *go*.'

'Tiger, this is giving me a rash.' He was scratching an itching palm.

'Where'd Sappho go?' Belle asked with concern.

'I sent them home, her and Willi.' He was transfixed by Belle's pleading eyes. They signalled urgency and have faith in me and let these two people go about their business and don't let me down.

Tony shook his head up and down slowly and without looking at Lady Molly or Uri said softly, 'Good night.'

Lady Molly squeezed his arm and said 'Bless you,' and she and Uri hurried away.

'I don't like any of this tiger. I love you and I trust you but I don't like any of this. What's going to happen to Sappho?'

'Come on back in. Liz has sobered up a bit. She can tell you what it's all about. She knows everything. She's always known.'

Inside Charlotte's cage, Flo was on the phone embroiled in an argument with an all-night garage. Charlotte was at the door and Belle responded to her anxious look with a reassuring pat on the cheek. Tony could see Liz, Pat and Malcolm huddled at the table in silence like mourners in a chapel. Gratefully he noticed steam rising from a cup of black coffee in front of Liz. Reba was softly crooning to Miss Toklas the parrot, '*Two in a million is lucky in lo-o-o-ove ...*'

Belle led the way to the table.

In the back seat of the Rolls Royce, Willi mustered the courage to break the tomblike silence she had endured from the moment the car pulled away from Charlotte's.

'Sappho?' Sappho dragged on her cigarette and exhaled a perfect smoke ring. 'What are we going to do now?'

'What is there left to do but pack.' She might have come to the decision to commit a mercy killing.

Willi repositioned herself cosily with one foot tucked under her. 'What about Babe?'

'Babe is finished.' The words tumbled about like cripples without crutches as Sappho quelled an emotion she could never share with Willi.

'You mean we go off and *leave* her?'

Sappho took a deep breath and replied to Willi's question with a strained effort. 'She would want it this way.

174

Babe is a good soldier. The best. She has always lived by the rules. This would be her decision if our positions were reversed. We've always had an understanding.'

Willi touched her arm. 'I think you're wonderful and brave.'

Sappho nodded gravely, the goddess accepting her due homage.

'Sappho ...'

'What?'

'The letter? Don't you care anymore about the letter?'

'It doesn't matter anymore. It's too late. Belle has the letter.'

Willi gasped and then asked, 'How did you find out?'

'Tony told me when you and Bale went looking for Babe.'

'You mean just like that he told you?'

'Just like that.' Sappho snapped her fingers for emphasis.

'But how *come*?'

'Because Pat Drake knew Pauline had given everything she took from me to Bale for safekeeping. You know how Pat prattles without thinking. Bale has the letter and she has even managed to decipher some of the words. Yes, you are quite right about her. Bale is a very clever girl. But I am still several steps ahead of everyone. By the way, we are not spending the night in the house.'

'Where are we *going*?'

'We shall pack and check into a motel near the airport. Our flight leaves at nine in the morning. Hugo,' she indicated the chauffeur, 'Hugo will look after us.'

'Hugo. So *that's* his name.'

'Is your passport in order by the way?'

Willi's face was a blank. '*What* passport.'

Sappho's sigh of despair sounded like a deflating balloon. '*Dumkopf!* How can you expect to leave the country without a passport?'

'Oh Jesus! Can't you *do* something about it? You can fix it up can't you. You can fix anything!'

175

Sappho said with resignation. 'I'll fix it up.'

When they arrived at the house, Hugo quickly got out of the car and opened the back door. As Sappho emerged, she said to the chauffeur, 'After you've locked up the car, come inside Hugo. I need your help.'

XI

Malcolm and Pat looked up gratefully when Belle and
Tony returned to the table. Tony positioned himself next to
Liz and asked, 'How you feeling, Liz?'

Liz replied with a sheepish smile, 'Like a brave old lady
facing a cowardly new world.'

'Ah nothing's that bad,' said Tony. 'I hear you got a few
things to tell me.'

'Oh Christ do I have to go through it again. Oh well.
Ours not to reason why.' She turned to Belle. 'Where do I
start.'

'Tell him what you saw at Pauline's.'

'Well Tony it wasn't all that much, believe me.' Liz
sipped some coffee and then sat back as she cleared her
throat. 'I didn't peep through any keyholes or listen at the
door. When I got there, the downstairs door was open so I
went right up. You know Bancroft, none of this where
angel's fear to tread crap. I ploughed right on up and heard
voices and I recognized all three. Lady Molly was telling
Pauline something and Pauline kept gasping "No" "No"
"Oh my God ... oh no" and then something like "Oh this
is too much ... here ... here ... take the keys ..." '

'What keys?' interrupted Tony. When presented with a
fresh can of peas, Tony wanted the identity of the label.

'The keys to Sappho's house,' Belle told him. 'Pauline
had a set.'

'How come?'

'Oh use your head. Willi has a set too. When Pauline
worked for Sappho she could come and go and set about her
job without disturbing anyone. When Pauline got her walking papers Sappho and Babe undoubtedly overlooked the
keys in all the hue and cry over the missing letter.'

'That's what Pauline said,' Liz interjected.

'What's with the keys?' asked Tony.

'We'll get to that in a minute,' said Belle, 'go on with the story Liz.'

'When I heard Pauline mentioning the keys, I brazenly entered the apartment. Pauline let out a yell and don't ask me why because I didn't look all that fearsome I don't think, She had a towel around her neck and looked positively awful. Come to think of it so did Lady Molly and Uri.'

Uri, thought Tony, not Mr. Bar Ishiba. *Uri.*

'Well anyway Uri made all sorts of angry noises about what the hell was I doing there and I said something about the letter and what the hell were *they* doing there and then Pauline screamed Belle's got the letter or words to that effect and Uri grabbed my arm and started to push me out the door. So I took a sock at him as we started struggling and then I heard Lady Molly saying something like "Stop it Uri ... stop it ..." and then Pauline made some ugly noise and Lady Molly said "Uri ... Uri ... the girl ... the girl". Well Uri for want of a better expression unhands me and there's Pauline lying flat on her back with her face looking a little purple and I rushed to her side and grabbed the towel which was now laying loose on the floor and started to dab at her forehead. Uri knelt and listened for her heart and said he thought she was dead and I started to feel sick. All of this couldn't have taken more then a minute or two.

'So brave little me says I'm going to call the police and Lady Molly takes over. She says to Uri "We must tell Liz everything" or words to that effect and of course I'm beginning to suspect the real reason Uri's in the country from past experience.'

'What past experience?' asked Tony abruptly.

'I'm getting to it. I'll tell this story in my own sweet way.' Malcolm sat with his hands folded on the table like an attentive student in class and Pat Drake wrapped an ice cube in a napkin and used it to sooth her fevered brow.

Liz continued with her eyes on Belle, 'The story Lady Molly told me didn't take long and I bought it. I bought it because I hate Sappho and I love Uri.'

'The past experience?' asked Tony.

'Yes. I met him in Israel years ago during the Eichman trial. We were introduced by a man named Simon Weisenthal. We fell in love and we had an affair. It's been going on ever since whenever we could get together which hasn't been too often. Yesterday he gave me my walking papers. I had a drink with him on the yacht and I took the goodbye like the brave little girl I am and after that I ran into Belle at that bar on Bleecker Street and almost poured it out to her then. Too bad I didn't. But what the hell, spilt milk.

'Anyway, I told Molly and Uri to beat it and I double checked Pauline after they left. I even tried the kiss of life and let me tell you it wasn't very pleasant. I've been drinking all day to wash away the taste. Why don't I ever get to give the kiss of life to somebody like Steve McQueen? All I got was Steve McDike. To continue, Pauline was positively dead so I split. I went to the studio figuring that sober atmosphere might rub off on me and then at some point I phoned your precinct and gave them the tip about Pauline.'

Tony had taken the crumpled notepaper from his pocket and was smoothing it out on the table top. He moved it in front of Liz and she studied it quickly. 'How neatly printed,' she commented.

'Thank you,' said Belle.

Liz read: '*You are in danger of the pursuit and judgement of the revenge sought by Bathsheba.*' A line had been drawn through '*Bathsheba*'. In its place, Belle had neatly printed:

'*Bar Ishiba*'.

Under '*Bar Ishiba*' was the hastily printed '*Wait*'.

Liz looked up and signalled thumbs up to Belle. 'You're a very smartie cookie, honey.'

'Save the compliments for later,' said Tony, 'who is Uri

Bar Ishiba? What's his bag?'

'He's a hunter,' said Liz.

'Yeah? Like what kind of hunter?'

'Like the aforementioned Simon Weisenthal who introduced us. They hunt for Nazi war criminals. Two of the biggest game they're after are a rat named Martin Boorman and a very nasty piece named Ilsa Lubin.'

Tony looked at Liz with incredulity. 'You telling me Sappho Yannopoulos is Ilsa Lubin?'

'That's what the lady's telling you,' said Belle.

Was it something I said?

Willi's eyes were wide with fear and her body was soaked with perspiration. She was back on the bed in the guest room, mouth taped, hands and ankles bound and thoroughly perplexed. Hugo the chauffeur had followed them into the house as ordered. She came upstairs to pack. The next thing she knew Hugo and Sappho came into the room and Hugo rushed her, pinning her arms behind her back.

And here I am!

Oh *Belle*, she thought through a whimper, were you trying to warn me about something like this on the street? Well why the hell didn't you come right out and say so?

Willi strained her ears. There was some kind of commotion going on downstairs. She heard Sappho yelling and sudden hope surged through Willi's veins. It's Belle! Belle trailed us back here! She's come to get me! She's come to rescue me! Good old true blue Belle! Come on Belle, come on up here and untie your little Willi and I'll be your slave for life!

After tying up Willi, Sappho had rushed to her suite with Hugo to get her belongings packed. There was the wall safe to be emptied of jewellery, money and private papers. Hugo had reminded her of the safe in the house in East Hampton but Sappho assured him there was nothing of importance there other than royalty statements from her publisher. In their feverish haste to collect Sappho's things, neither Hugo nor Sappho heard the stealthy activity on the floor below.

With Pauline's keys, Uri Bar Ishiba and five crewmen from the yacht *Jason* had entered Sappho's house. On the street behind the grey Rolls Royce was parked the innocent looking delivery van in which they had arrived. In the rear of the van Lady Molly was hidden to serve as a look-out.

Uri and his confederates had entered the house with practised caution. He deployed two men to check the downstairs rooms and they soon returned with a reassuring report. Uri started to ascend the stairs when he heard a movement and quickly signalled the others to secrete themselves. Hugo came down carrying two suitcases followed by Sappho, her arms laden with furs and one hand clutching a jewellery case. When they arrived at the foot of the stairs, Uri stepped from behind a curtain and said simply, 'Ilsa Lubin'. Sappho screamed and Hugo dropped the cases and lunged at Uri. The five crewmen immediately materialized. Two overpowered Sappho and the others made short work of Hugo with the help of a monkey wrench firmly applied to the base of his skull. A chloroformed pad was held tightly over Sappho's nose and mouth until she gracefully sagged like a prima ballerina in the closing moment of *The Dying Swan*.

Hugo was dragged to a closet, shoved inside and the door was locked and the key removed. Uri went to the front door, opened it a crack and swiftly reconnoitred. Three crewmen scooped up the furs, jewellery case and luggage. Three minutes later, the delivery van pulled away from the front of Sappho's house with Uri at the wheel. Twenty minutes later, it arrived at the Seventy-Ninth Street boat basin. When the contents of the van were transferred on to the yacht, Uri went to Lady Molly, took her in his arms and kissed her passionately.

'Am I forgiven?' he whispered.

'Uri darling, I always knew only a small part of you would ever belong to me.' She tweaked his nose and added with an irresistably wicked levity, 'But it's my favourite part.' He kissed her swiftly and then rushed up the gangplank. '*Bon voyage*,' said Lady Molly and then climbed behind the wheel of the delivery van and drove off in search of a likely place to abandon it.

While Operation Ilsa Lubin was underway in Greenwich Village, Tony Mingus was bristling with indignation in *Checkpoint Charlotte's*. 'But if I don't phone this in to the precinct, we're all accessories to the crime of *kidnapping*!'

'Sappho's no kid,' snapped Belle.

'I don't give a damn who she is or what she is. I'm a cop and I'm morally obligated to try and stop it.' He raced to Charlotte's cage and the telephone. Belle pushed her chair back to go after him but Liz grabbed her hand.

'Sit down and have another drink, honey. Put your money on Uri. They can send the harbour police after the yacht, but by the time they catch up with it, Sappho will have been transferred to another boat. I know how they work and they do it beautifully. Anyway, whatever happens, Sappho's finished.' She reached over and appropriated Pat's drink and raised it high. 'Here's to the end of *Sappho's Sisters*! And oh have I a beautiful scooperoo for tomorrow morning's programme!'

'Oh Gahhhhd!' moaned Pat.

'You got the curse, honey?' asked Malcolm with feigned sympathy.

'Think of all the disillusioned women across the country tomorrow. Just *think*! Oh oh oh!' She was twisting her napkin until it looked like a garrot. 'I can just see the smirk on Norman Mailer's face.'

Belle guffawed and then suddenly brought herself up short. 'Jesus Christ! You don't suppose they took *Willi*?'

Liz Bancroft doubled up with laughter while Belle left the table to pose her question again to Tony.

Grimly relaying his information into the telephone in an insistingly loud voice, Tony was unaware of the sudden

182

hush that fell over his immediate vicinity. For the first time in years, Charlotte's corncob pipe dropped out of her mouth and Reba the bartender gripped the counter with a sudden attack of the vapours. There was an exchange of a variety of perplexed and astonished looks among the clientele at the bar as Belle arrived at Tony's side.

'Tony!' Belle hissed in his ear, 'Tell them about Willi!'

Tony said 'Wait a minute' into the phone and then put his hand over the mouthpiece. 'What *about* Willi?'

'Supposing they took *Willi* along with Sappho!'

Tony pursed his lips. 'That almost tempts me to forget the whole thing.'

'She'll be so unhappy in Israel. She can't stand Jewish food.'

Tony removed his hand from the mouthpiece and alerted the detective on the other end of the phone to the possible abduction of Willi Horn. '*Wait* a minute,' he said again into the phone and then turned to Belle with a look that told her she just might be an idiot. 'What the hell would they take *her* for? If that Uri is all that smart, he's up on his international law. She's probably trussed up back at the house.' He returned to his conversation with the detective at the precinct and told them he was going down to Greenwich Village to investigate Sappho's house.

Back at the table, Pat was continuing to bemoan the fate of Sappho's disillusioned followers. Liz said drily, 'Don't worry too much, honey. Germaine and Kate and Betty and the others will take up the slack.'

Belle returned to tell them she was accompanying Tony to Sappho's town house. She zeroed in on Liz, 'Keep yourself available to make an official statement tomorrow.'

'And what about dear Lady Molly? Are you so sure at this very moment she isn't sporting a yachting cap and swallowing some dramamine?' Liz as the woman scorned was entertaining her private vision of Lady Molly on the vessel of wrath.

Belle leaned across the table. 'Any bets? I'll cover all

183

takers. My money's on Lady Molly. She'll be around tomorrow to finish the story. Why don't you all go home and get some sleep.' With that suggestion she left them to join Tony who was waiting in the unmarked car with Detective Kelly and the others.

'*Sleep!*' exploded Pat Drake. 'She's got to be joking! My adrenalin's at full boil!'

'You know. I hate to admit it,' said Liz with a far away look in her eyes, 'you have to hand it to Sappho. She certainly must have recognized Uri's name tonight from Yannopoulos's letter. Yet I gather she sat at this table with him as calm, as cool, as collected as. . . .'

'. . . a goddess,' whispered Pat. 'Oh what the hell you have to give her that.' A beatific expression settled on her face. 'Her bright flame was a beacon for so many of us and who can deny if only for a brief moment, she was an inspiration. Why that simpering look on your face, Malcolm?'

'I was just wondering,' he said frivolously, 'has Doctor Joyce Brothers considered changing her name to Doctor Joyce Sisters?'

Upon arriving at Sappho's town house, Tony was not surprised to find the front door unlocked. He hurried in with Belle, Kelly and the other detectives behind him. An overturned table and a hall rug askew were the only signs of a struggle. 'Check the downstairs,' Tony barked to Kelly as he took the stairs two at a time, Belle nimbly following.

Willi's face was blotched with tears when they found her. Tony said to Belle, 'I told you Uri didn't want any excess baggage.'

Willi's eyes were blinking rapidly as Tony set about untying her. Belle tore the tape from Willi's mouth and Willi screamed. 'Oops! Sorry!' said Belle with the sincerity of a cannibal biting into a missionary.

Willi glared at her and hissed, 'What *kept* you.'

Willi never suspected how close she came to another sock

184

on the jaw. From downstairs Kelly was yelling, 'Hey Mingus! We found us a pigeon in a closet! He's been sapped! He says he's the chauffeur!'

Tony's face lit up like a lighthouse beacon in a storm. 'Just what I was hoping for! A witness to the snatch! Come on Belle, we're taking the two back to the precinct.'

Willi scrambled off the bed and went skittering after them. 'Belle! Belle! What's to become of me? Where will I go?'

Belle paused at the head of the landing and placed her hand on the newel. She nailed Willi with an icy look, drew herself up with dignity and said in a beautifully simulated southern accent, 'To tell yuh the truth mah dear, I don't give a damn.'

The ensemble returned to the precinct where Tony immediately requested the necessary papers to hold Hugo and Willi in temporary custody. The desk sergeant told him, 'There's a lady waiting in your office. She said she was *sure* you wanted to see her.' He emphasized 'sure' in an embarrassingly bad British accent. Fairy lights of joy were twinkling in Belle's eyes as Tony led the way to his office.

Lady Molly was seated in a straight-back wooden chair with her monocle firmly fixed in her eye scanning the early edition of the *New York Times*. A cigarette holder dangled from the corner of her mouth and smoke spiralled up from the butt it held. She looked up when they entered, removed the holder from her mouth and said gaily, 'There you are! And Belle too! How perfectly lovely! My cup runneth over!' Belle felt like a latecomer at an embassy reception. 'I phoned before coming and your lovely sergeant said he was sure you'd be coming back here and I decided there was no time like the present to clear up this matter. Have I done the right thing?'

'I hope you are about to take a large load off my mind,' said Tony as he sat behind his desk. Belle made herself comfortable in a chair next to Lady Molly and wondered

185

aloud if Tony could scare up some coffee. While Tony translated her suggestion into an intercom, Lady Molly took Belle's hand and squeezed it warmly.

'Whatever the consequences, Belle, I wish to thank you. I thank you very much. Why do you look so concerned? You're not worried about me, are you? Not to worry my dear, not to worry at all. My embassy is always prepared to deal with these little scrapes I get myself into. It's happened several times before, you know.' She crossed one leg over the other and smoothed her dress while Tony caught a good look at her shapely legs and realized here was indeed a very handsome woman. 'There have been similar adventures with my late husband. Sadly enough, that's how I lost him. In Africa, I believed I mentioned that didn't I?' Belle nodded. 'Only Uri and I escaped. One is never too sure where betrayal lurks. But this one went off like a dream. It was touch and go. Of course, I never suspected Sappho would turn up at Charlotte's tonight.' Tony and Belle were transfixed and were barely aware of a policeman entering and depositing on Tony's desk a tray that held three plastic cups of instant black coffee.

Lady Molly continued as she watched the coffee-bearer depart. 'One does have to admire how she brazened the evening out, doesn't one? I watched her face when I said "Bar Ishiba" and she never flinched. Remarkable, isn't it? But then, she didn't know how close you had come to the truth when you deciphered those words and nearly hit on "Bar Ishiba" with "Bathsheba". Hmmmm.' Her face became a study briefly. 'I wonder who that Bathsheba was my poor darling dallied with in Haifa.' She looked up with a twinkle in her eye. 'Uri does have a voracious appetite for women. Well why not, he's only human although there are those who will give you an argument on that score. No sugar in my coffee, thank you, Tony.'

Tony served the coffee and then turned to his desk. 'I heard Liz Bancroft's story. Now can we hear the rest?'

'Well actually, what Liz has told you is exactly what

happened in Pauline's flat. What Liz didn't realize is that Pauline was in dreadful pain from the injury she'd received to her neck. Poor little thing. Poor little thing. She flitted about like a trapped canary.' She now favoured Belle. 'When we got there, Uri and I were unaware she had turned the letter over to you. That was the first we knew about it. But I did know she possessed the keys. I learned that at breakfast. We wanted those keys because it would simplify the mission. Sappho's house was wired with electric alarms and Uri prefers to avoid that sort of thing wherever possible. You Americans have so many new, mysterious systems.' She turned to Tony. 'Sappho's abduction wasn't planned for tonight. It was to happen tomorrow. Uri was that positive the letter would be in his possession. You see, we had to be *sure* Sappho was really Ilsa Lubin. There have been two earlier and rather embarrassing mistakes which proved to be rather expensive.' She sipped her coffee and grimaced and then quickly wiped the grimace from her face when she realized it was impolite.

'By the by, Belle, I'm sure you'll forgive Uri but your office has been ransacked.'

Belle said wearily, 'Be my guest.'

'It didn't occur to us of course that you had the letter on your person. How wonderful you had it with you at Charlotte's.'

'I knew what I was doing, Lady Molly. When I deciphered the four words and the name, I had a pretty fair hunch what you might be up to. When you mentioned the yacht and Uri's name ...'

'You'd heard it before?'

'Oh no. It meant nothing to me. But "Uri" somehow had the flavour to match "Bathsheba" and I began to get an idea as to why Sappho was a marked woman.'

'A very marked woman. Let me tell you about Ilsa Lubin. I'll make it brief and then you'll understand why the Israelis were determined to bag her. Ilsa is a Pole and before her country was overrun by the Germans, foresaw that inevitability and became the mistress of a German agent. She was in her early twenties then and quite a ravishing creature. She'd been a film actress in Warsaw but an extremely minor one. But she went the full route as this German's mistress. Espionage, betrayal, you name it she did it. For her services, she was rewarded a woman's concentration camp as commandant. That's were she met Babe Lustig, Hilda Frobe actually. I needn't go into the figures but you can be well aware of the amount of murders she perpetrated and condoned and not, I assure you, on order of the high command. She ordered wholesale slaughter the way other women deal with their greengrocers. Among the victims were Uri's mother and two sisters.'

Tony added more sugar to the muck in his plastic cup and Belle was sitting forward with hands clasped around her knees.

Lady Molly lit a fresh cigarette and continued. 'When the war was ending and the Russians got into Poland, they captured Ilsa Lubin. Babe escaped to Switzerland somehow. Ilsa Lubin was brutally beaten and disfigured. She wasn't killed because the Russians kept a large reserve of prisoners for exchange. With the help of confederates in Switzerland, Babe engineered Ilsa's release. In Switzerland, she underwent a *cure*.' Lady Molly hadn't planned intentional levity at that moment but Belle laughed. 'Yes, I suppose it does sound funny. But I suppose "cure" is as good a word for it as any. She had plastic surgery and gave herself a new identity. She laid low for several years, making her plans, and no need for me to remind you that we have been dealing with an extremely ingenious little beast. She emerged on the French Riviera around nineteen forty-eight or so with Babe. Ilsa and Hilda were now Sappho and Babe. Sappho had lots of money, beautiful clothes and jewellery and secure that her new face, her new identification would never be penetrated. And why not? She had new papers and birth certificate and you name it, she had it. Those people are so good at arranging things like that.

Sappho lusted for fresh power and set her sights for the biggest game she could get.

'You'd be amazed at the men she tried to lure. And then into Nice sailed dear little Nikos Yannopoulos. Man of mystery, recluse, and terribly terribly lonely. Sappho maneuvered to meet him and the rest is history. He did have her investigated but her new background was flawless. So he married her. Nikos was a friend of my husband's and so I met Sappho Yannopoulos. Of course all this time Ilsa Lubin is still on the Israeli's wanted list and they are working like beavers attempting to trace her along with all the others. Sappho's biggest mistake of course was having Babe in constant attendance. There was *no* disguising Babe's origins, but Sappho couldn't do without her. She loved her too deeply. And Nikos of course was a good many years older than Sappho, in his sixties then, and not making too many demands on Sappho's sexual favours if any at all. Sappho bided her time for almost two decades, amassing wealth and of course private information concerning a good deal of Nikos's own suspect manipulations and when the time came, left him and struck out on her own.'

'He let her go just like that?' asked Belle.

'He had no choice. Sappho was in a position to blackmail him and had her information carefully stored away in Switzerland to be released should Nikos attempt revenge. Sappho and Babe left for this country where of course she pounced on the Women's Lib movement as just her meat. The Israelis meantime were on the scent of three women who might be Ilsa Lubin, one of them Sappho. The other two as I told you turned out to be embarrassing mistakes. After my husband's death, my relation with Uri as you have well gathered deepened, and as I was acquainted with Nikos, I was assigned to his end of Sappho's trail. Poor old thing is practically doddering you know, almost senile, but he kept his silence. One of Uri's agents infiltrated Nikos's network and by now most of his incoming and outgoing mail was double-checked. Undoubtedly I aroused Nikos's

189

suspicions. He knew about me and Uri and hence that letter to Sappho. Always on those cheap, innocent looking air forms. Well my dears, that brings us to the present, doesn't it? By the process of elimination, Sappho was our girl but we needed the proof. She was now too large in the public's eye for there to be a slip-up and a mistake might have caused havoc with their other similar endeavours.

'Well!' She slapped her knee and looked at Tony with a mixture of pride and defiance. 'Uri's got Sappho and soon she'll be making fresh headlines!'

'Lady Molly, speaking for myself,' said Tony sincerely, 'I hope Uri gets through. But I have to tell you, I've alerted the harbour police to the yacht.'

Lady Molly smiled. 'If they're looking for the *Jason*, they'll have a hard time tracing it. There's a new name on the yacht now. And by now,' she glanced at her wristwatch, 'Sappho has been transferred to another ship. Happily, I have been kept in the dark as to its identity. I can't help you there!'

Tony shook his head in a gesture of admiration. 'I got to hand it to that Uri.'

'Oh yes, Tony. You've got to hand it to that Uri. You might just as well. He'll take it anyway.'

Thirty minutes later, Lady Molly Burke was safely deposited at her borrowed apartment by Tony and Belle. Belle and Lady Molly made a date for lunch the next day to be followed by a visit to Bergdorf-Goodman and Korvette's, and then Tony took Belle back to her apartment. There Tony phoned the precinct and learned that Babe Lustig had died. Hugo's statement confirmed what they knew about Sappho and there was the question of what to do with Willi who was undoubtedly a hapless innocent. Belle suggested, 'Put her on ice.' Tony ordered Willi's release.

Belle poured them each a nightcap and they sat on the sofa holding hands. 'How about it, tiger,' said Tony gruffly.

190

'How about what?'

'Marry me.'

Belle stared into her glass for a moment and then said, 'Let me sleep on it.'

Tony snuggled up to her. 'Why don't we sleep on it together?'

To Belle's amazement and subsequent delight, they did.